Alternate Rialto

KIMBERLY MENOZZI

Published by: Good to Go Press

Alternate Rialto

ISBN: 0615491561
ISBN-13: 978-0615491561

Per Alessandro.
Ti voglio tanto bene, per sempre…

1

Ypsilanti, Michigan was nothing like this. For that reason alone, Emily Miller knew the scene before her should have been perfect. Beyond the Basilica di Santa Maria della Salute, the sun faded from the sky. Streaks and splashes of orange, pink and red darkened and drained down into the sea. The water of the lagoon deepened to violet and then to indigo at the base of the dock – *the Molo*, she corrected herself – while the black-and-white striped shirts of the gondoliers glowed ghostlike over the sleek black boats drifting silently toward the Bridge of Sighs.

With a little imagination, it would be easy to be lost in a fantasy of timelessness and forget that it was Nineteen-Ninety-Eight. Forgetting the past year – or at least to forget the last six months or so – would be a blessing, anyway.

The breeze off the water swept the fringe of short hair off her forehead and out of her eyes. Loose strands from her ponytail tickled and danced delicately along her neck. Her skin went gooseflesh for a moment in the cool air after the sunset, but it was a relief to have the baking heat of another July day over and done with. Now she could cease fanning herself, relax and watch the crowds from her seat here at the café with her friend, Jenn.

A jumble of voices and a burst of laughter by the water drew her attention. Her gaze shifted to a group of young men and women laughing, chattering and playing along the edge of the Molo. She watched, smiling, as they feigned attempts to push one another into the water next to a cluster of docked gondolas.

As the group came closer, she saw they were younger than she had first thought. They were teenagers, barely old enough to be out of school. One of the boys grabbed a girl by the hand and swung her wildly about, until, squealing with laughter, she teetered on the edge of the walkway. He pulled her back, put his arms around her and planted a kiss on her still-laughing mouth.

For a moment, Emily fancied she could feel that same sort of kiss on her own lips. It hadn't been so long ago since Jason had kissed her that way, had it?

A sense of guilty voyeurism swept over Emily before she looked away. She swallowed hard, her throat rasping with an aching familiarity. Breathing deep, she caught the salty tang of the lagoon, tinged with just a hint of something green – mold or even mildew, perhaps. Another, gentler breeze carried the scent of strong black coffee from a couple of tables over, making her mouth water for the bitter taste.

It was all too beautiful. Too perfect. Too...Venice. A custom-ordered sunset, a cool breeze, beautiful people everywhere. Her imagination hadn't overhyped anything, after all. She wished that Jason would leave her thoughts long enough for her to enjoy it.

If only he hadn't promised to bring her here. If only he hadn't promised to love her forever. If he'd only kept one promise – just one. Her hand settled briefly on her abdomen before she pulled it away.

Twenty-five years old and she already felt like an old maid.

Then she noticed the handsome blond stranger, in white linen, who stood with his back to the sunset. His gaze was focused on Emily's table.

Or, rather, his gaze was focused on Jenn.

As usual.

It was only natural. She glanced down at her own plump figure, then over at Jenn's classic Nordic features. Not for the first time,

Emily considered the fact her statuesque best friend was uncommonly attractive.

Rather like the man who was watching Jenn now.

Emily sighed, picked up her Bellini and took a cool, peach-infused sip. Jenn had insisted on ordering them although Emily didn't drink much alcohol.

"And so, I manage to avoid even the charms of Venice," Emily mumbled, resolving to ignore her friend's admirer.

Jenn turned toward her, away from the passersby strolling along the Molo toward Piazza San Marco. "Come again?" Her long, elegant fingers pushed her sunglasses up to rest above her forehead.

"Nothing, Sissy." Emily directed her gaze back to her drink, helpless to stop picturing the stranger. "I was just thinking aloud."

"Do tell, Mouse." Jenn said. She leaned forward, gesturing with her free hand toward her friend's head. "What's going on in there?"

Emily took another sip of her drink and turned to watch the blond stranger again. He was gone.

"I guess I've just been a bit lost in my head. I keep thinking about…stuff."

Jenn frowned, tilting her head to one side. "What's that? What are you thinking about? Jason?"

"Yes, and no. I mean… Look." Emily put her drink down and faced her friend. "Two weeks we've been here. Rome, Pisa, Florence, and you've had a…*boyfriend* in every one of those towns, and I've had nothing. Nada. Zip. Zilch. Not so much as a *whiff* of genuine interest."

"Oh, you exaggerate."

"Not a glance, a pause or a 'how-do-you-do?'" Emily continued, sitting back.

"You've had plenty of glances, you know. Besides, maybe there isn't an Italian equivalent to 'how-do-you-do', anyway. I mean, besides '*come sta?*'"

"Don't be facetious. It doesn't change the fact that my last hope has just been dashed," she paused to permit a peach-flavored hiccup, "to bits."

"Stop being so melodramatic." Jenn glanced around and focused on her friend again. "What do you mean, 'dashed'?"

Emily focused her gaze on the dark outline of the railing where the handsome stranger had been. How best to explain that she'd been foolishly pinning her last romantic hopes on this city's charms as their tour of Italy wound down?

Weren't Italian men supposed to be positively *crawling* over the female tourists? She'd been counting on them to help cast Jason Hastings forever out of her memory.

Further, she was thoroughly unmoved by the city itself. After the excitement of planning a trip to fabulous Italy, arriving at Fiumincino Airport in Rome had been an anticlimax; and a messy, troublesome anticlimax, at that. The arrival in Venice two weeks later felt somehow lackluster.

When they'd gotten off the train and crossed the piazza in front of the station to board a *vaporetto* to their hotel, Emily had been unimpressed. Even the Basilica di Santa Maria della Salute, which she had always wanted to see, gave her only the dimmest flicker of a thrill. It was there, right in front of her, and it meant nothing – or next to nothing. It might as well have been an amateurish backdrop for a high-school play for all the excitement it stirred within her.

Yes, Venice was romantic in the way all the ancient cities of Italy were romantic. On this trip she'd filled countless rolls of film with shuttered windows, colorful landscapes and crumbling, moss-covered stairs. But there were no clandestine embraces, no stolen kisses, no enticing gazes from handsome men meant for her. There were no deeper memories behind the images to give meaning to what she saw.

Heck, I probably won't even bother developing most of them. What's the use in a thousand photos of landscapes and buildings, when I've already forgotten half their names?

"Earth to Emily." Jenn waved her hand close to Emily's face, drawing her out of her ruminations.

"I've had enough." Emily finished her drink and put the empty glass on the ceramic tabletop with a hollow *clink*. "I'm going back to the hotel."

"Why don't you tell me what's really wrong, first?" Jenn leaned closer under the still-open umbrella over the café table.

Emily caught another glimpse of the handsome stranger. Once again her throat tightened painfully. He was coming their way. She couldn't bear to witness the scene playing out as it always did, with her watching from the sidelines. Better to give her friend at least a modicum of privacy.

"I'm tired, that's all. Besides, I think you've got a date," she said, and walked away.

The crowds thinned considerably in the evening hours. Emily had no trouble making her way through the remaining clusters of tourists and residents.

She slowed as she followed the winding, narrow alleys to her hotel. The scent of dampness clinging to concrete came and went, depending on the whims of soft breezes meandering their way along with her. She and Jenn saved money by staying further away from the touristy locales. Now Emily could appreciate the distance in a different way as she strolled through the residential areas. The silence closed gently around her and allowed her to think.

Enough time had passed for her to feel a bit guilty for how she'd addressed Jenn at the café. It wasn't her friend's fault things hadn't gone well. That was like saying it was Jenn's fault that they were so different.

Short and tall, dark and light, round and slim, Em and Jenn. In spite of the differences, they were best friends from the day they met in grade school, when Emily's family had moved to Michigan from Indiana. The girls had grown up together, gone from middle school to college together, and now had undertaken their first international journey together.

Jenn always drew all the attention from men, it was true. There was no changing the fact. Besides, what else could be done? Stop being friends because she wasn't getting any of the spotlight? Wouldn't that be totally, utterly selfish? Obnoxious, even?

She paused in front of a *pasticceria* and examined the goods in the window, vaguely considering if she should get something to take back to the hotel. Even at the far end of the picture window from the open door, she smelled the sweet aromas of powdered sugar and flaked dough. And yet, there was little temptation to buy a sack full of pastries – with her virtually non-existent Italian, who knew what she'd actually end up buying? The idea of consoling herself in stereotypical fat-girl style, while Jenn doubtless would have the handsome stranger up for a different sort of nightcap, was even more depressing.

She tried to allow herself to imagine stopping their friendship cold, and how it would make her feel to do so. A sudden sense of emptiness shook her at the thought. No, it really was unthinkable. Sure, it was possible to give up her best friend, but what would be the point? Why cut off the one real friend she'd had in her whole life? Why give up the one person she'd been able to open up to after her father died and Jason had turned out to be such a jerk? Just to spare herself the occasional sense of rejection from strangers?

"This, too, shall pass," she said under her breath to her reflection in the *pasticceria* window, and imagined Jenn admonishing her melodrama again. She resumed walking, turned a corner and found herself in Campo Santa Marina, her hotel tucked away in one corner. She rang the bell, pushed open the door when the buzzer sounded and trudged up the stairs to the front desk.

The receptionist on duty was a young man around her own age. He barely glanced in her direction after he'd verified her ID with her room information. With an air of indifference, he handed over the heavy brass key attached to a burnished wooden block. She ran her thumb over the number engraved in the wood, the edges of it polished smooth by countless hands over the years.

"*Buonasera*," Emily said, making her best attempt at Italian with one of the few words she felt comfortable using.

"*Bonaséra*," the receptionist mumbled, never taking his eyes off the television and the scantily-clad girls dancing across the screen.

Same as always, Emily thought, resisting her urge to wave her hands in front of his face with a sarcastic "Hello...?" Instead, she rolled her eyes then toyed with her key as she walked along the narrow hallway to her room.

After showering until the water had gone tepid, she dressed in fresh pajamas and got into bed to find a lump under her pillow. She slid one hand tentatively beneath and fished out a collection of romantic short stories, no doubt left there by Jenn that evening while Emily freshened up before dinner. She thumbed through the well-worn pages and then set the book aside on top of the bedclothes. Instead, she picked up her much battered and beloved copy of *The Master and Margarita* from where she'd left it on the nightstand.

Jenn had spent most of their flight from the US teasing and entreating her to read something different. "Nothing like a little light reading, eh? Russian literature? Why not a book about Italy?"

"I'll be *in* Italy," Emily answered.

"Give up and give in to *Italia*!" Jenn cried, over-enunciating the last word in a feigned Italian accent. "Have an adventure! At the very least, why not read something that will set the mood for you? Like a guidebook or something?"

Remembering, Emily shook her head, smiling a little, even though the exchange on the plane and her friend's relentless enthusiasm had been exhausting.

Emily picked up Jenn's book and held it up to the light from the bedside lamp. Inexplicably, Jason's face flashed through her memory.

"Why not, you ask?" she asked with a sour twist of her lips, then tossed Jenn's book toward the desk. "Because that book is full of crap."

8

2

Dreamlike, watery voices drifted and echoed, calling to each other and reflecting off the walls in a language Emily didn't understand. Dull splashes followed, accompanied by jeering, teasing shouts before the rumble of an engine rattled the windows in their frames for a moment. She squinted through sleep-heavy eyes and behind the fine lace curtains of her window made out a woolen grey sky over the rooftops of the next building.

She spied Jenn's book resting on the floor next to the wastebasket, and she fumbled out of the bed to retrieve it and place it on the small desk in front of the window.

I'd rather not forget it there in case Jenn shows up early.

Undressing as she went, she padded barefoot across cool marble tiles into the bathroom. Not for the first time, she was thankful she and Jenn had separate rooms. After the intense togetherness of traveling, it was a distinct relief to have a little time alone. It could be lonely sometimes, though, without the chance to chat late into the night like they did in their dorm room.

But I always have hot water, and I don't have to wait for Jenn to finish her beauty routine.

She eased herself under the steaming spray of the shower and adjusted the temperature to a more endurable level. Her humming echoed off the tiled walls as she rinsed away the suds and luxuriated under the pelting water.

They had no set plan for the day, save an aimless stroll around the city after breakfast, but she had hopes of photographing everything possible. She intended to use up all of her film before getting on the plane, if only to prove her mother wrong for having said she'd never need all the rolls she'd bought. She only had a handful left, after all, so it shouldn't be a problem. Maybe they could go to Murano? Or Burano? She wanted to get some shots of the lace makers and the glass makers, too, if she could. A few "mood pieces," perhaps? And maybe –

A muted *thump* cut into her musings, followed by another, and then another. From the other side of the thin wall, familiar laughter reached through the noise of the shower: Jenn and her male companion. Emily froze in the warmth of her own shower, feeling icy all over save for the rush of heat to her ears and cheeks.

Oh, geez...

Shutting off the water she stepped out and wrapped herself in a towel. The scene formed in her mind's eye, unbidden – Jenn and the blond stranger of the night before making love in the shower, the natural wake-up refresher for the morning after.

She saw it all with a disturbing intensity – the water running over his shoulders, soapsuds cascading down his back and sides. However, she imagined her own hands sliding across his soap-slicked skin, struggling to grasp hold while she wrapped herself around his tawny form –

Emily bit her lip and sat on the bed, toweling her hair roughly, not caring that she was still wet from the shower. While she struggled to push the image of the blond stranger from her mind, the sounds of Jenn's exultations continued – faint, but undeniable.

The rush of blood in her ears soon covered everything else. Clutching the towel closed around her torso, she crossed to the wavy-glassed window over the desk and fumbled one-handed with the lock until the window creaked open toward her. The sound of a passing outboard engine drowned out any noise from inside the hotel. With a grateful sigh, Emily sank onto the chair at the desk.

She tucked the towel tightly around her chest and moved to sit on the edge of the desktop. The lace curtains shifted lazily on the breeze while she peered out through the delicate designs at the canal below. No gondoliers there, just normal, average Venetians going about their lives.

One shutter swung on its hinges with a rusty squeak as another breeze pushed at the curtains and carried a hint of the morning's warmth into the room.

On the gondola ride she and Jenn had taken the day before, the gondolier told them all about the history of the city, the romantic legends of Casanova and the charmingly decadent traditions of *Carnevale* masked balls. They had toured beneath the Bridge of Sighs and past the home of Marco Polo himself, with Emily dutifully snapping photos all the while.

More than once, the briny smell of the water had made her a little nauseous. Especially when the dead rat had floated by – or rather, when they had skimmed past it. Of course, the gondolier had flirted outrageously with them both until the ride was over. She had expected as much, really. Listening to other gondoliers touring other women was enough to prove this was all part of the experience. The way he had become polite with Emily and lingered tellingly to assist Jenn out of the gondola and back onto the dock was par for the course, too.

The smell of salt and musty damp wafted past her and she flinched before forcing herself to breathe deeply in spite of the tangy, fishy smell. One keen ear trained toward the bathroom, a flash of guilt warmed her as she listened for his voice. The thumps had ceased, and the rumble of water through the pipes had stilled. She went to her suitcase to pull out a few things to wear, dressing in the silence and ignoring the lump in her throat.

When she stepped out of her room at last, she heard Jenn's laughter at the end of the hall, in the hotel's breakfast room. Emily locked her door and braced herself for a meeting with Jenn's paramour. She wondered what he would look like up close, if his eyes were blue or brown, and if he was as handsome as he'd seemed at a distance. She'd soon find out.

Upon turning the corner Emily stopped short, even though Jenn smiled sunnily and waved her over. Unsteady legs carried her to her friend's side, where she waited, briefly uncertain if she should sit with Jenn and her companion, or at an adjoining table.

It took time to sink in. The man's eyes were brown and so was his hair. No question about it, this was not the mystery man who had been watching Jenn the night before, but someone else altogether.

Emily bit her lip for a moment before forcing an anxious smile.

"Good morning." Jenn singsonged, extending one hand toward the man sitting across from her. "This is...Matteo. We met last night." The momentary hesitation before his name wasn't lost on Emily.

"I know," she said, clearing her throat and adding quickly, "I mean, um, yeah. Hi, Matteo."

"Matteo, this is my best friend, Emily." Jenn said, still beaming.

Matteo nodded politely in her direction.

"Did you sleep all right?" Jenn asked.

"Oh, sure. Yeah. I found your book, though."

"Did you?"

"Uh, huh." Emily nodded and looked at Jenn, still hoping against hope. "So, what do you want to do, today?"

"Well, um... You see, Em... Matteo and I... Well, we thought we might spend some time together today, instead. Maybe take a gondola ride."

Emily noted the way that Matteo's dark eyes, with their ridiculously long lashes, lit up for just a moment when Jenn said his name. In that moment, with his clear complexion and black curls, he seemed much more like a boy than a grown man.

"That certainly sounds interesting," Emily said, pushing uncharitable thoughts aside and turning so only Jenn could see her face. "I'm sorry, but could we talk for a moment, in private?"

Jenn's face fell for an instant before she regained her sunny expression. "Of course."

Emily led her outside the breakfast room and into the alcove next to the front desk.

"What's the problem? You don't like him?" Jenn's tones were measured and soft, calm as ever.

"Does it matter if I like him? You're going to dump me again – just blow me off like our plans are nothing, aren't you?"

"What are you talking about?"

"Look," Emily began, folding her arms across her chest to hide her trembling. Her throat was positively aching, now. "Look; in Rome, when you stayed out all night with Sandro, I didn't complain, did I? In Pisa, I didn't fuss when I had to climb the tower by myself while you went off with Carlo; in Florence I happily toured the Uffizi alone while you saw Lorenzo instead. But you *promised* me we'd hang out together today."

"Oh, come on..." Jenn rolled her eyes before making a quick gesture toward the breakfast room. "I mean... Did you *see* him?"

"Yes, I *saw* him," Emily said, Matteo's dark eyes and curls flashing through her mind. "I got a real good look. And I heard him this morning too, you know."

Instead of embarrassing Jenn, as she'd hoped, the statement only seemed to straighten her friend's spine and cool her gaze.

"You have a problem with that?" she asked, her words slow and measured.

"Yes – no – I mean –" Emily stammered, taken aback. "I just–"

Jenn sighed deeply, pressing one hand to her forehead. "I don't know what to say. I thought we came over here to have some fun, didn't we?"

"Well, yeah, of course we did."

"That's what I'm doing. So why aren't you?"

"Like it's my fault?" Emily's protest erupted a bit too loudly and she paused, swallowing hard. "I'm not the one who's dumping her friend every time some good-looking guy gives her the eye."

"Maybe you would, though, if you'd ever let yourself notice that someone is *looking* in the first place. Jesus!"

Emily blinked hard, surprised at the tears that burned behind her eyelids. "That's just evil. That's so not fair."

"What do you mean?" Jenn leaned in closer, lowering her voice so Emily had to lean in, too. "How am I being unfair?"

"You know men don't look at me. Not like they look at you."

Jenn stepped back from Emily, folding her arms across her chest. "Mouse, hon… What do you want from me?" She raised one hand as if to silence any retort Emily might give. "You need to lighten up and just... I don't know. You need an adventure, don't you? Just give in and *have* one. Today, pay attention. I promise you, the attention will be all yours."

With that, Jenn turned on her heel to walk back to the breakfast room and Matteo. Emily followed a moment later, pretending not to notice when the couple passed her on their way out. She sat at a table and dabbed at her eyes with the sleeve of her blouse. The hostess came out of the small kitchen and gave her a warm smile, placing a basket of bread and jam on the table.

"*Caffè? Tè?*"

"Tea, please," Emily answered quietly, falling silent before her trembling voice could betray her. This was as close as she had ever come to having an actual fight with Jenn, and now she was at a loss for what to do.

She ate her breakfast in silence, occasionally looking out the window at the *campo* and the people milling around there.

I'll go out and about, today. Kill time in some way and have lunch somewhere, even if I am alone. I can totally do this.

"I need an adventure, she says," Emily muttered to herself, then realized that she was alone in the breakfast room. "I wouldn't know an adventure if it walked up and bit me on the nose."

3

Emily drifted from one *campo* to another, taking photos almost at random. A doorknob here, a dilapidated-looking bridge there, yet nothing compelled her to study these subjects deeper. One angle, one shot and she moved on. It was too much trouble to focus and get past what initially met her eye. Despite all her best efforts, her thoughts kept returning to Jenn and Matteo, who were doubtless getting to know each other better.

I should have kept my mouth shut. What point was there in saying anything, anyway? How foolish I must have seemed, protesting like a jilted girlfriend. What is wrong with me?

Jason's face flashed through her mind again, and her cheeks flushed with heat. She pushed the thought away and passed one hand over her face to wipe away the perspiration.

She shook her head and paused atop a bridge to watch a pair of gondolas pass at the end of the canal. Raising her camera she framed the shot, feeling a momentary embarrassment for taking such a "touristy" photo.

Ah, what the hell? Why not? It's not like I'll ever come here again.

Another gondola passed beneath the bridge a moment later and she stilled herself, waiting for the perfect image. An errant breeze lifted her skirt just as the gondola emerged. The gondolier looked up at her, and Emily dropped her free hand down to protect her modesty. His blue eyes flashed with mirth at her reaction before he turned back to focus on the task at hand, taking his crooked grin out of her view.

She couldn't resist the smile that tugged at the corners of her mouth before she crossed to the other side of the bridge.

Finally, a reaction that's just for me - but only because of a panty-flash? That figures.

Emily wandered down a *calle*, listening to the incomprehensible snatches of conversation from behind closed or nearly-closed shutters, the clank of pot lids being replaced, the thuds of what sounded like a knife on a cutting board. She sniffed at the elusive scents of broths and butters wafting out from each home. A perverse mix of familiarity and homesickness clutched at her for an instant, even though she knew it was impossible for her home to be more different from these.

The idea of her mother standing at a table cutting and dicing vegetables for dinner curved Emily's mouth into a bitter grin that she struggled to erase.

Turning a corner she stepped out into a large *campo* with a distinctly forgotten air to it. The buildings were like most of the others in Venice, with faded paint and exposed bricks casting the dreary grey light down to reflect off the paving stones. The café was still closed, chairs and tables made of aluminum and wood stacked haphazardly upon each other and chained together in spite of the approaching lunch hour. Flaking green shutters, the only flashes of color in the square, remained closed to the late morning light.

She framed the details and snapped away, the sound of the camera loud in the emptiness.

The window of a shop selling ceramic and cloisonné jewelry caught her eye. She positioned herself carefully and took a few photos of the goods on display. She smiled again, feeling a flash of hope that the photos would turn out well. Looking around, she noted another shop, this one with postcards and prints displayed on boards by a door below street level.

Two steps down and she was inside a paper shop. She busied herself putting her camera away while looking at postcards in a spinner rack, admiring the photos and watercolor impressions of *Carnevale* and "typical" Venetian scenes. She was alone, save for the elderly proprietor. He remained seated behind a counter piled high with handmade notebooks, art prints and blank sheets of paper.

Emily acknowledged him with a shy nod and continued browsing, feeling conspicuous in a quiet broken only by faint, tinny music from the radio on the shelf behind the man. She bent awkwardly to examine posters on the broad table in the middle of the main room without touching them, holding her camera bag back to keep it from knocking things askew.

Two images in particular held her attention; one, a print of the bridge at the other end of the square, with the arched doorway and two oval windows in the background; the other, a sketch of Proserpina dining on the pomegranate seeds that doomed her to return to Hades every year.

She looked at the sketch, thinking of her father and how he used to read to her from a picture book of Roman myths. She'd loved the way his warm voice brought the stories to life for her, changing for every character, giving each their own accents and tones.

Proserpina – Persephone in the original Greek tale – had always been one of her favorites. Autumn and winter were Emily's favorite seasons, and the idea that they'd been created from Ceres' longing for her daughter gave Emily a strange melancholy. Her own father would have missed her hard enough to bring the winter, she knew. Her mother? Not likely.

Her book had contained the version of the tale where Proserpina had willingly eaten the pomegranate seeds, to ensure she could stay in Hades. Emily was a teenager before she realized what this had really meant. Proserpina could always cry off, saying she'd been tricked into eating the food of the dead – she hadn't meant to, not really. But return she would, all the same, to fulfill her obligations.

Shaking her head, Emily paced around the table to look at the other prints. She returned to the print of Proserpina, but her thoughts drifted now to her stubborn disenchantment with Italy in general, and Venice in particular. Had she overhyped the whole journey for herself, or were other forces to blame? Jenn's excitement and intensity had been a great deal of fun – at first. It was only later when it had worn thin. She'd insisted on learning more Italian than Emily could ever manage and then used it at random opportunities, even before they'd left the States.

Her repeated hawking of romantic books hadn't helped, either. All the time she'd insisted it was for Emily's benefit, to help her get over Jason. According to Jenn, three months was plenty of time to recover from a breakup, but still...

And if I'd had to listen to one more Pavarotti CD, I'd have had a fit.

Emily wandered into another section of the shop, finding a display of stacked blank sheets of paper. She picked up one sheet and ran her finger and thumb against the grain, feeling the roughness as though from a distance, through numb fingertips. Handmade, no doubt. It didn't feel strictly "papery" at all. She thought how pleasant it would be to sit with this paper on an easel, a box of watercolors on her lap, painting one of the scenes in Piazza San Marco. It would be pleasant, that was, if she actually painted.

"*Signorina, posso aiutarLa?*"

Emily hesitated, turning toward the man behind the counter.

"Huh?" She put down the sheet of cloth-like parchment she'd been examining and tried to still her trembling hand. Damn Jenn for leaving her to deal with this on her own.

"Um... *Non capisce Italiano bene, scusate...*" The words stumbled out of her mouth and she cringed, heat flooding her cheeks.

I know I've made a bunch of mistakes, there. This guy will think I'm an idiot and throw me out of the shop, now.

The shopkeeper smiled. "*Ha visto qualcosa che lei piace?*" he asked, gesturing toward the prints, and then to the blank paper.

She put her hands in her pockets so the shopkeeper couldn't see them shaking, and he picked up the parchment paper she'd just put down.

"Was I not supposed to touch it?" She looked around but didn't find any signs like those she'd seen in the mask shops, which read "*Non Toccare*/Do Not Touch."

His cloudy blue-green eyes held her in foggy regard.

"*Lei è Inglese?*" he asked, as the bell over the shop door made a muted chime.

"Um..." She felt almost ill, and shoved her hands deeper into her pockets.

"He is asking if you are English, *signorina.*"

"What?" Emily turned toward the new speaker and found herself staring up at the handsome blond stranger from the Molo the night before. Only now, rather than white linen, he was dressed in an elegant suit and tie which seemed out of place in the faded and musty surroundings of the shop.

It couldn't be him, *here, could it?*

"He is asking if you are English," he repeated with a smile.

"Does he speak English?" she asked hopefully.

"Ask him," the stranger insisted, with obvious amusement.

"Um... *Parlo-?* No, wait... *Parli inglese?*"

The old man's smile warmed still more at her attempt. "*No, mi spiace.*"

Emily frowned and glanced around the shop. Her hands were still shaking in her pockets and now her whole body had begun to tremble.

"I'm sorry," she said. Color rushed to her cheeks fast enough to make her dizzy. "I'm sorry," she repeated, and edged past the stranger to hurry out the door.

She paused at the top of the steps then set off for the bridge at the far end of the *campo*. The sound of footsteps behind her followed a moment after.

"*Signorina? Signorina?*"

Emily forced herself to stop and turn to face the smiling stranger who was crossing the *campo* in amiable pursuit, his blue silk tie flapping in the breeze. An image of Pepe le Pew bouncing after the object of his affection came to mind while she watched his unhurried approach.

"You left this back there," he said, offering a scroll of paper tied with a purple ribbon as he stepped up to her.

"You're very kind, but, that isn't mine." She took a step away, busying her hands with her camera bag.

"Isn't it?" He glanced down at the object still in his hand. "Are you certain?"

"Positive," she said, then walked away, her heart pounding so hard she could barely think.

"Oh, no... You mean that...?"

Something peculiar in his tone made her stop and look back at him. He stood with the scroll clutched close to his chest, an expression of exaggerated horror on his face.

"Quick! Don't let him catch us – he's faster than he looks!"

Emily watched in bewilderment as he hurried to her side.

"*Signorina*, have you ever been in a Venetian jail? They're terribly humid and miserable and I don't recommend the experience."

"What are you talking about?"

He waggled the scroll in his hand, careful to keep it hidden between them. "I thought it was yours, so I took it to bring it to you."

"Oh!" She cast an instinctive glance toward the shop. The handsome stranger's mouth quirked just the least little bit at this, and she knew that she'd been suckered. Emily nodded to begrudgingly acknowledge his efforts and raised one hand in a farewell gesture. "Cute. Funny. Goodbye, now."

"Please, wait." He held the scroll out once more until she felt compelled to stay. "This is yours."

"I didn't buy it."

"I did."

"Why?" Emily took another step away from him, eyeing the scroll in his hand.

"I have no idea. I just thought you should have it, after I saw you admiring it in the shop." He offered it once more, and she reached hesitantly to take it.

Emily untied the ribbon, the purple silk sliding with a whisper against itself in the silence of the square. Something about the ribbon made her blush; the almost liquid sensation of it beneath her fingers seemed somehow suggestive. It was enough that she swiftly tied it once more into a simple bow and thrust the scroll back into his hands.

"I can't accept this, I'm sorry." She saw him primed to protest and she raised her hand to stop him. "I don't know you. I've seen you once in my life before now, and you appear out of nowhere and give me a gift? How can I possibly think that's okay?" A flash of realization struck her and her spirits sank. "Besides, I know why you're doing this. You want me to introduce you to Jenn. Well, you're too late. I'm afraid she's found someone else to spend time with. Next time, you'll have to act a little faster. Sorry."

His bemused expression gave her pause before she turned on her heel to depart.

"I'm not sure who you are talking about, *signorina*," he called after her, "but you certainly seem to set much shop by her."

"I what?" Emily stuttered to a stop at the entrance of the *calle*.

"You 'set much shop' by this person." He spread his hands out in a gesture of confirmation, still holding the scroll. "You think much of her."

"Oh, I see. I think you mean I 'set much store' by her." She watched him with narrowed eyes, wondering what he would say next. "I guess I do, at that. But come on, it's obvious, isn't it? I saw you watching our table last night, on the Molo. You were watching her."

"No, I wasn't." He moved to join her, his gait still unhurried.

"Of course you were. Everyone watches Jenn."

The stranger shook his head, an amiable grin spreading across his mouth. The humor of it touched the corners of his eyes as he offered her his free hand.

"My name is Jacopo Spadon."

She took his hand automatically, cursing his handsomeness a moment later. He'd pulled her right in with that, hadn't he?

"Emily," she said, trying not to stammer. "Emily Miller."

"Emily," he repeated, pronouncing her name "Emmy-Lee."

With his accent, her name almost sounded exotic.

"Emily Miller, it's nice to meet you. Would you do me the honor of joining me for dinner this evening, or must I chase you across this city again?"

At once, she pulled her hand out of his and stepped away from him. "Excuse me?"

"I saw you when you arrived last night, and I decided to make your acquaintance. As it turns out, however, you are a very hard person to get close to."

"Why?"

"Why what?" He tilted his head to one side in a disarming gesture.

"Why do you want to 'make my acquaintance'?"

"Do I need a reason?"

What do I say to that?

"I guess not," she said and attempted a nonchalant shrug. "Let's just say it's a mystery to me, then."

"All right, a mystery it is. But do you accept?" He leaned toward her, just the least little bit, and a faint breeze brought the scent of his cologne to her.

For a moment, she could taste it on the back of her tongue. A blush rose promptly to her cheeks at the surprising, intimate sensation, as though she had just kissed him and tasted his skin for herself.

This is crazy. What am I doing, talking to this man? This man who I've already pictured naked, just a few hours ago...

She recalled her fantasy in detail and blushed, her hand rising swiftly to her face to hide it. Startled by her sudden gesture he drew away, and with her blush intensifying, she took a belated step away from him.

His smile returned and she forced herself to calm down, praying that her anxiety wasn't obvious.

"Just give in and have an adventure," Jenn had said.

Well, why not? And if it turns out that he wanted Jenn instead, I can deal with that, can't I? I just won't get my hopes up.

"Emily? Hello?"

Jacopo's gentle voice prodded her back into the present. She cleared her throat and gave him a shaky smile.

"I accept," she said, and felt the familiar rush of warmth to her cheeks once again. "I'd like to have dinner with you, this evening."

"Wonderful. Where are you staying?"

"At a hotel in Campo Santa Marina," she answered, and wished immediately she hadn't said so. It might have been better to meet him at the restaurant.

"All right, then. I will meet you there at seven o'clock, is that agreeable for you?"

"Yes, that would be fine."

"I will see you tonight, then, Emily Miller."

She nodded and turned away, trying not to rush down the *calle* away from him, for fear of giving him the wrong impression. Or worse still, the right one.

4

Sunset was still some time away, but the shadows of the buildings surrounding the *campo* created a premature sense of dusk. Emily stepped out of the hotel to search in the last light for Jacopo.

There was no sign of him, yet. That was as she'd expected.

She settled on a stone bench in the last of the sunlight. At first, the light opposite blinded her and she raised her hand to shield her eyes. Soon, however, she dropped her hand to her lap and fussed with the skirt of her sundress and her small purse, picking away imaginary lint.

He wouldn't come. It was crazy to believe even for a moment that a man that good-looking could possibly be interested in her.

A glance at her watch showed her plan of being "fashionably late" had failed. He was late instead, by nearly twenty minutes.

Before she knew it, she drifted into her sometime daydream of living somewhere far from home – Jenn called it her "expat fantasy." Her mother preferred to dismiss it as a "coward's way out." A weight settled on her chest and pressed toward her spine until she drew a long, deep breath to make it disperse.

Just a few more days, and I'll be home again.

She hated the fact that the thought filled her with such dread, but she couldn't help it. The return to her mother's haranguing and criticism – without her father there to act as a buffer – was something she couldn't escape. Then it would be back to school and work, and having to pretend that it didn't bother her to see Jason there, every day.

She wound her hands in the strap of her purse, making a garrote of the leather between her fists.

"Emily, there you are!"

Oh, my God. He's actually here.

He stepped up to her, smiling in apology.

"Forgive me for being late, but it couldn't be helped."

He extended one hand to her and she took it, permitting him to draw her to her feet. She trembled and hoped it was imperceptible; how humiliating would it be if he saw the effect he was having on her, already?

Still holding her hand, he stepped away and gave her a swift once-over. A blush rose from her throat into her cheeks at his obvious appraisal.

"*Che bella,*" he murmured, half-turning her from side to side. "Shall we go? I have a table reserved for us at eight. I know you Americans like to eat early."

Emily gave her best nonchalant shrug.

"I don't mind a late dinner, so long as I don't have an early morning." She clamped her mouth shut, resisting the urge to cover it with her hand. To her surprise, Jacopo laughed and nodded.

"I agree; a fine dinner is best enjoyed without an early morning. But the reservations are already made."

He took her hand in his own once more and led her toward the canal behind the hotel. A runabout, moored at the end of the small dock, bobbed gently on the small waves left by a passing motorboat. The soft *swop* of waves slapping the underside of the dock and the sides of the boat was somehow soothing.

Still, she hesitated at the sight of it.

Am I crazy? I'm hopping into a boat with a man I don't know from Adam, in a city I've never been in before. Anything could happen now. How does Jenn do this?

He released her hand when they reached the runabout. Emily steeled herself for an awkward descent, hoping that her soft leather sandals wouldn't somehow betray her. The dock seemed to rise and fall beneath her feet as she fixed her gaze on the boat; her stomach made a mild, momentary lurch at the illusion. Inhaling deeply, she rested one hand on a piling and watched Jacopo remove the mooring line and jump into the boat.

He extended his hand to her and noted her hesitation with a single raised eyebrow.

"Are you okay?"

"Fine, fine... I'm just a little, um, awkward getting into boats, sometimes."

The corner of his mouth quirked, as though at some enjoyable memory.

"And so you came to Venezia. Do not worry; I won't let you fall in. *Infatti*, I will make sure that you do not. Just step on the side and in, like on stairs."

"Easy for you to say."

"Trust me, Emily. There will be no problems if you do as I say. You will be okay."

Emily drew another deep breath and accepted his proffered hand.

"Step down now," he said. The statement had the air of a command, and she did as he said without hesitation. Jacopo's hands, suddenly secure at her waist, pulled her toward him, lifting and settling her into the boat with ease.

The boat rocked beneath her feet while her heartbeat slowed to a rate that would let her breathe. Jacopo's hands still held her, offering support and reassurance.

"Sorry," she said, hoping her quiet words would carry above the sound of the water lapping against the boat.

"For what?"

"I don't know, really." Emily shook her head, unable to look him in the eye. "I just feel silly, I guess."

She placed one hand on the edge of the windscreen to steady herself before she settled into the passenger seat. Jacopo sat with one arm draped casually over the backrest of the pilot's seat.

When at last she raised her eyes to his face, she found him smiling. Still. His ice-blue eyes were full of laughter.

"You'll get used to the water, Emily. Don't worry."

"Maybe. I only have a couple of days left, anyway." She faced forward and pretended to smooth a wrinkle in her skirt. "Will that be enough time?"

"More than enough, I'm sure," he said.

Something in his tone made her turn to face him, curious. His face was unreadable in profile as he started the engine and pulled them away from the dock.

Once underway, the breeze swept his hair back from his face, the honey color fading to white gold in the flashes of light reflecting off the windows of the palazzos lining the canal. Every so often he would turn to her, his eyes crinkling with unspoken mirth.

"So, where are you taking me?"

"A little place I know. You'll like it."

Making course adjustments with almost careless gestures, he slalomed through the narrow canals as they bore east, toward the lagoon. Emily resisted the urge to swallow a momentary rush of panic before the thought of more open waters calmed her. The zigzagging and deceptive near misses would end soon enough.

They didn't speak. She turned her focus to the ancient, weathered buildings that rose from waters which lapped over once-pristine entryways. Every so often she caught a whiff of mold or damp, the salty tang of the sea or the brackish aftertaste of stale water drifting on the air from dilapidated docks and waterlogged piers.

The air freshened as they neared the lagoon, and Emily had an impression of a genie freed from a bottle when the runabout emerged from the narrow canal. Jacopo's skin took on the golden cast of the sunset, bespeaking health and long days spent outdoors.

Emily couldn't help thinking of her own pinkish colors, exaggerated from the days she and Jenn had spent touring around. Sunscreen was terribly unreliable, and more than once on this trip she'd returned to the hotel to soak in a cool bath or shower to reduce the burn she'd gained from her day's sojourn.

Her pale limbs looked quite sickly, indeed, in contrast to Jacopo's healthy color.

He took the runabout along the Molo, past the gondola docks in front of Piazza San Marco and onward. Emily watched for the café where she and Jenn had sat the night before, when Jacopo had watched them.

Watched me. *He said he watched* me.

They sped steadily on toward the Grand Canal, where the last of the sunlight daubed the Santa Maria della Salute in shades of tangerine and pomegranate.

Emily didn't hide her gasp at the sight, nor could she resist turning to look back while Jacopo steered them up the canal without pause. Her pulse thumped with a solid insistence in her chest, until it resonated throughout her entire body.

This is how I was supposed to feel yesterday – or during the whole trip, for that matter.

She caught Jacopo watching her again. He turned away but his smile dazzled, even in profile. Her heart stuttered and she raised one hand to her breast, as though he might see the flutters and it would give her away.

Was this a sign, then? Should this mean something to me?

Before she could contemplate the possibility much deeper, the roar of the engine died down to a softer rumble. Jacopo steered them to a piling along the foot of the Rialto Bridge, glowing soft pink and purple above them in the early evening light.

"Emily." His soft voice carried above the sounds of the crowd to feel like a caress in the relative silence after the engine's shutdown. "Let me help you up."

Stone steps ascended from the water to the walkway, and Jacopo's steadying hand kept her from losing her footing on the slippery surface. Once on the pavement he held her hand secure in his own, placing his other hand at the small of her back to steer her along the bridge.

In spite of herself, she was compelled to pause at the top and push through the crowd that had gathered along the wall to have their photographs taken with the Grand Canal as the backdrop. She wished that she had brought her camera with her, but smiled to think how silly her bulky camera bag would have looked with her outfit.

"*Che peccato*," Jacopo said, taking her hand and drawing her away from the wall. "What a shame. If only we had a camera to make your photo."

Her eyes widened at the statement.

"Besides," he continued when she remained silent, "this light is quite flattering to you." His smooth fingertips slid from her hand to her wrist and back again. "It is like your skin is made of roses."

The thudding of her heart had to be noticeable; it was thumping so hard in her chest. Emily had a vision of his lips on her wrist, just grazing there before continuing along her arm, and she shook her head to dispel it.

This is going to be quite an evening, I'm sure of it.

Her silence didn't seem to disturb him in the least. Jacopo gazed wordlessly into her eyes for a moment before he took her hand in his once more and led her off the bridge. He guided her down a darkened *calle*, full of twists and turns, until she lost all sense of direction in the coming dark.

5

They stopped in front of a narrow, dark doorway. A slab of wood hung to one side, a makeshift blackboard with a list chalked on it. None of the words made sense. They bore only a vague resemblance the Italian Emily had seen throughout her tour.

"Peseera dee oro," she mumbled aloud, reading the wooden sign above the doorway, and Jacopo chuckled softly. "What does that mean?"

"*Pesièra dé òro*," he read, his fluid accent sounding almost Spanish instead of Italian. "It's in our dialect. It means 'Kettle of gold'." He held the door open and indicated that she should go inside. "Don't worry, Emily. I will order for you."

"Okay." A sudden apprehension shook her when she stepped inside the cool, dimly lit restaurant. Her eyes were slow to adjust to the darkness as she waited for Jacopo to take her arm and guide her to a table. A painfully thin man stood at the far end of the room, indicating the way with familiar, easy gestures.

The man spoke an incomprehensible mix of babbling dialect and broad pantomime as Emily and Jacopo took their seats. A single small candle cast a cheerful glow from the center of the table, giving just enough light for her to see Jacopo's flashing smile. The two men continued gesticulating and talking loudly, ignoring her for the moment.

To think, I'd nearly allowed myself to believe I'd understand Italian, one day.

She resigned herself to grasping absolutely nothing and allowed her attention to wander, picking out small details in the gloom. There were none of the usual tourist trappings in view; no harlequins or *Carnevale* masks, no miniature gondolas or reproductions of the Santa Maria della Salute, no sterile or forced romantic mood-setters. Indeed, there were no tourists in the place.

The simple plaster wall felt cool against her shoulder and the crazy-paving of the floor lay pleasantly uneven beneath her feet. Two simple water glasses, flanked by two smaller ones of similar design, rested upside down on either side of the candle, reflecting the light in their liquid sheen. The rough wood of the table was evident beneath the thin, pale pink tablecloth. The mismatched plates and heavy silverware, which bore the patina of years of service, proved this establishment was well off the tourist path.

Emily soon realized that she was the only American present. For that matter, she might have been the only American to ever come inside.

The host stopped talking, turned on his heel and went into the kitchen. A brief flash of light illuminated the back of the dining area as the door swung open and shut on silent hinges.

Jacopo folded his hands on the table and focused on her again. "So? What do you think?"

"Um... It's interesting. I've never been in a place like this, before."

"Of course you haven't. Sadly, it is difficult to find real food here in Venezia, unless you know where to look."

"Are most places like this, though?"

"No. This is a favorite of mine. It's very traditional, and tourists do not come here."

"Why not?"

"Would you have come in, if I hadn't been with you?"

Emily thought about the sign above the door, and the menu chalked outside.

"No, I suppose not. I wouldn't have understood any of it."

Jacopo nodded as though she'd said something profound. "*Sì, sì.* Other tourists don't come in, for the same reason."

"So, is he getting the menus?"

"I have already ordered. You like seafood," he said, more a statement than a question.

"Well..." Emily blushed, grateful for the dim lighting. "I'm not a fan, really." Jacopo's expression darkened, becoming almost unreadable. "But I can always try something, of course," she added. "I'm sure it will be good."

"It will." His cheerful demeanor returned. "I told you Emily. You don't need to worry."

"I'm not worried." Her smile wavered on her face for a moment before she willed it steady.

The host returned, flipped all the glasses on the table upright and placed a corkscrew and a bottle of wine down with a *thunk* before he turned and rushed away. There were only a handful of other patrons in the tiny establishment.

Jacopo turned the bottle of wine, reading the label with great care in the candlelight before applying the corkscrew with a clatter and a soft *pop.*

After he poured a glass and took a sip, she watched him purse his lips, pause, then swallow in the smooth, practiced efforts of a vinophile. A single nod of his head pronounced that the contents were acceptable, and he proceeded to fill Emily's glass just over halfway.

I thought people only did that in films.

His gaze was steady upon her while she cleared her throat and reached hesitantly for her glass, then took a timid sip

"So, Emily," he began, "you don't drink wine, either?"

"No, not really."

"Would you prefer something else? A Coca-Cola, perhaps?"

She felt a flicker of anger at his playful, mocking tone, but suppressed it.

I'm probably being oversensitive, anyway.

"No, Jacopo, I'm fine. It's just that I'm not used to wine, at home. Many Americans aren't, I think," she added. "At least, not in my family. It'll take some getting used to."

"But it is good, no?"

"Yes, I suppose it is."

Jacopo sat back in his chair with a quiet, satisfied sigh and an enigmatic Cheshire-cat grin.

The host returned a moment later with a bottle of water that fizzed as he opened it. He poured a splash into the larger glasses before putting the bottle down and hurrying away once more.

Emily took a grateful sip of the sparkling water, even though she didn't care for the tonic aftertaste that followed the bubbles. Now that her eyes were better adjusted, she noted the prints on the walls, hung in weather-beaten old frames. They looked very much like prints she had seen in the paper shop that afternoon, and she turned to ask Jacopo if he knew anything about them.

Instead, when she faced him again, she was startled into silence. His gaze seemed almost predatory, until his disarming smile defused it a moment later.

"Tell me something about you, Emily. How did you come to be in Venezia?"

"Oh, it's just a vacation, really. Jenn and I decided to come when she won the contest."

"Contest?" he echoed.

"Yeah. Jenn works at a travel agency in Ypsilanti–"

"Eep...?" he interrupted, looking puzzled.

"Ypsilanti, in Michigan," she explained. "Jenn sold the most holiday packages in a month. She got two free tickets to a European destination, and since she always wanted to come to Italy, here we are."

"You didn't want to come to Italy?"

"It's not that I didn't *want* to, I'd just never thought about it, one way or another."

"But what do *you* do, Emily? *Parlami di te*. Tell me about you."

Emily cleared her throat, fussed with her plate and then took another drink of her water. "Well, I work part-time at a book shop off campus. I'm in school. I'm studying Journalism and English Literature."

"You're still in school?"

"Yeah. I took a couple of years off after high school, so... since I've only gone part-time, I'm still in school at 25." She shrugged and focused her attention on the candle's flickering light. "I know how it looks, trust me."

She forced herself to face him again and found a distant expression had stolen across his features. *Oh, God, I've bored him silly already*, she thought, taking in his glazed eyes and his hands folded in front of his mouth in a pensive gesture.

"It doesn't look bad, Emily. Not everyone can go to school and be an all-time student."

A small smile stole across her lips at his mistake, but she said nothing about it.

"Thanks. At any rate, that's how I got here – riding my best friend's coattails." She bit her lip. "So what about you, then? What do *you* do, Jacopo Spadon?"

"It's boring," he offered with a dismissive shrug.

"Tell me anyway."

"I work in a bank. I've worked there for seven years, since I was your age."

Emily wondered if he could tell she immediately did the math.

"I travel a lot, but it's not a glamour job. I get to see the country and sometimes I go to England and I get to practice my English." Jacopo took a long sip from his wine glass.

"You're very good," she encouraged with a smile. "How long have you been speaking English?"

"You hear many tourists speaking it in Venezia, so it is good to know. I learned some when I was younger, so I could give directions to lost people or tell them the time, but to properly speak it, I had to take courses. I have studied it since ten years. I started studying in University, because it is so common in banking."

"I can't imagine that."

"What?"

"Needing to speak another language on a daily basis for work, or living somewhere I'd need to know another language so well."

"You wouldn't consider it? If the opportunity arrived, you would not live somewhere else?"

"I didn't say that." She reached for her wine glass to gulp a bit down. "I just don't know how I'd cope with living somewhere that different."

"I suppose you would adapt. That is what people do, isn't it? We adapt, even to situations that are not to our liking, sometimes only to please another person."

Emily studied his face, but the low light made it difficult to read his expression, and her hasty swallow of wine had her head swimming.

"You're probably right about that."

"I am." Jacopo's eyes held hers over the flickering candlelight. "So, Emily... It is just you and your friend traveling? Why isn't your boyfriend with you?"

Pushing her reflexive scowl off her face at the word "boyfriend," Emily shrugged. "I don't have one."

"No boyfriend? Your lover, then."

His bluntness threw her. How was she supposed to answer that?

Her gaze fell to the tablecloth and she fussed with the placement of her cutlery to avoid meeting his eyes. Cheeks burning, she took a deep breath and spoke.

"No lover, either."

Their host rushed out of the kitchen and set a serving plate between them. Emily noted the assortment of appetizers with a wary eye.

Jacopo picked up her plate and placed a few items on it before handing it back to her. "*Capesante, aringa affumicata, patè di fegato,*" he recited, pointing at each in turn. "Scallops, smoked herring, veal liver patè."

She regarded the offerings for a long moment before reaching for the patè. *Might as well try something new.*

He filled his own small plate, then ate with his eyes on her all the while.

"No lover?" he asked, continuing as though there hadn't been any interruption.

Emily selected the herring and stuffed it in her mouth. She nodded, then shook her head, unsure of the proper response. Jacopo's smile embarrassed her further and the familiar heat rushed to her cheeks again before she swallowed.

"Nope. No lover. You?" She asked this last with a bravado she wasn't sure she felt. She swallowed another sip of wine and wondered if maybe that was why.

His only answer was a sly grin.

They continued eating in silence, and she caught his assessing gaze sliding over her yet again.

The host swooped in to spirit away the empty plates, returning with fresh ones and another two full plates to share between them. "*Bigoli con l'anara,*" the thin man said, putting down the plate of pasta and sauce. "*Casumziei ampezzani,*" he added, setting another plate of half-moon-shaped pasta next to it.

"Pasta with duck sauce, and cheese ravioli with poppy seeds," Jacopo explained, dishing out portions as he spoke.

The host watched them both for a moment, then fired a question at Jacopo. The only word in Jacopo's response that Emily thought she understood was "*americana.*" The host turned and left in his usual abrupt manner, disappearing behind the kitchen door.

"What did he say?" she asked once she was sure he was out of earshot.

"He asked why I was explaining the food to you in English." Jacopo waved his hand dismissively. "I told him you were American."

This course was much easier to enjoy. Emily savored the flavor of both pastas equally, though the rich duck sauce won her over just a bit more than she'd expected. When she reached for her wine glass, she found it empty. Jacopo immediately filled it to the rim.

"And you said you do not like wine?" he teased, putting the bottle back on the table.

Emily giggled behind her hand. "Who knew?"

"Indeed. But then, I must say that we never know what we are capable of until an opportunity arises. Life is surprising in this way."

She nodded, considering this statement.

"Life is definitely surprising," she affirmed, and couldn't help smiling again.

"To Life, and its surprises," Jacopo proposed, raising his glass of wine, and she took her own in hand as well.

"To Life, and its surprises," she echoed, touching her glass to his, and the tiny chime shimmered between them in the quiet of the dining room.

6

The streets were virtually empty, the *campi* deserted. They crossed the Rialto Bridge again, Jacopo guiding her as before, but this time he steered her to a place at the wall. The bridge was aglow, the ghostly pale stone surface softly illuminated by strategically placed lights. They stood and looked out at the reflections on the water which rippled, rose and fell with soft, gentle lapping against the boats moored nearby.

"Emily," he said, his voice scarcely carrying above the soft murmurs of conversation around them. She drew her gaze away from the hypnotic dance of light on water to face him.

Yes? she wanted to ask, but the word never formed on her lips. Instead, his hands framed her face and held her still as he brought his lips to hers in a soft kiss. She raised her own trembling hands to cover his as he kissed her again. At once, the other people vanished, along with the bridge, the water and the city itself.

His hands slipped from under hers to stroke her hair, tangling in the length of it while his kiss deepened. Her heartbeat was distant and remote, somewhere else. There were only his lips, parting hers and lingering while he pulled her to him and held her securely in his embrace. Emily trembled as eagerness, anxiety and need warred amongst themselves, threatening to breach the surface at any moment.

An adventure. I need to have an adventure. I deserve it, too, don't I?

Awareness of her surroundings filtered through, murky and submerged but slowly clarifying in the laughter and soft talk all around them. At last, she opened her eyes to find herself looking directly into his. The pale, summer-sky blue of his eyes held her transfixed for what seemed like forever.

"Is this the part when I wake up, then? I think it usually is," she murmured, the thought unintentionally spoken aloud.

"What?" Jacopo asked, his brow furrowing in puzzlement. His embrace relaxed but he didn't release her.

"Nothing," she said. His direct, sustained gaze intimidated her, and she cast about for something else to focus on, if only for a moment. Soon they were both gazing out at the water, watching gondolas and other boats pass at leisure beneath the bridge.

They stood silent for a long while. Other couples came and went, taking their turns to gaze out at the Grand Canal. With his fingers twined in hers, a thrumming energy twitched in his fingertips. She had the impression that something more was supposed to happen, that he was waiting to act on some plan unknown to her.

Now I'm just being paranoid.

Still, she couldn't quite shake the feeling.

"It's time to go," he said, tightening his grasp on her hand. "I'm sorry, but I have to work in the morning."

"Oh," she said, trying hard to keep the disappointment from ringing too clearly in her voice.

Of course. So much for the adventure. Unless...?

She erased the thought before it could form in the depths of her mind. There was no point in setting herself up for a fall.

Once more, Jacopo's hand found the small of her back and guided her through the waning crowd toward the boat waiting at the dock. They went more slowly this time and Emily cast cautious glances in his direction, trying to read his expression in the come-and-go lighting before they turned onto one of the smaller canals.

Her thoughts drifted and she daydreamed him pulling the boat to one side to kiss her again; her mouth went a bit dry at the thought.

Furtively licking her lips while pretending to watch the scenery, she willed her mind to stop racing.

I suppose there was something he didn't like about our kiss on the bridge. Maybe I didn't respond well enough? But what did I do wrong? Why didn't he want another one from me?

With some effort, she managed to calm herself. To her surprise, she found he was already tying the boat to the dock behind the hotel, as if she'd slept the last part of the journey back.

Damn. So much for committing it to memory, then.

Neither of them spoke as they walked to the hotel, his arm around her waist keeping her close. The only sounds were the rustling of her skirt, the soft clapping of her sandals, the somewhat more solid tapping of Jacopo's shoes against the paving stones, and the murmur of voices in the night from the open windows of the surrounding homes.

At once, she felt sleepy and cozy, likely a side effect of having the wine with dinner. The lulling warmth of the night folded itself around her, snug but not cloying. Emily thought that, if he asked her to, she could walk alongside Jacopo like this the whole night through.

All too soon, they were in the *campo*. Emily watched Jacopo cast curious glances around them before she realized that she hadn't told him which hotel was hers.

"Well," he said, taking her hands in his. "Here we are. Shall I walk you to the door?"

Emily nodded, not trusting herself to speak.

Should I ask him up? What would he think of me if I did? Is it too much, too soon? I went out with Jason for a month before we did anything – but I don't have a month, here. Heck, I don't even have a week!

"Which one is yours, Emily?" Jacopo asked, a soft chuckle beneath his words.

She indicated with a tilt of her head, suddenly shy, before she could force the words out.

"Over there."

Jacopo nodded and took her hand to lead her up the stairs. To her surprise, he accompanied her inside and up to the landing for the hotel. Outside the door he took both her hands in his again and gave her a warm smile.

"I had a good evening, Emily Miller." His voice was quiet in obvious deference to the silence of the building. "I trust you did, as well?"

"Yes," she answered without hesitation. "Yes, Jacopo, I've had a lovely evening."

"*Bene...*" He nodded and then cleared his throat. "I have to go; I have an early morning, so..."

Emily nodded her understanding, suppressing a mental curse at the same time. Before she could speak, Jacopo released her hands and stepped closer, once again framing her face in his hands and kissing her with a surprising tenderness.

Determined not to make the same mistake as before, Emily returned the kiss in kind, meeting his efforts while he pressed closer still. She wanted this, wanted *him*, and she knew this opportunity was unlikely to present itself again.

It was difficult to think and soon she abandoned the effort, giving in to his kisses and offering her own.

Somewhere on the edge of her consciousness, she was aware of the sound of footsteps climbing the stairs to where they were. Why worry about getting caught? She was a tourist, destined never to see this place or these people ever again.

Jacopo certainly wasn't about to be distracted. His own eagerness and excitement was all too evident when she pressed close to him, and not only in the way his hands tangled in her hair or clutched at her waist to hold her against him.

Never in her life had anyone kissed her like this. She could smell the wine, slightly sour and earthy, mingling with his sweetly-clean breath with each kiss. His lips tasted salty and warm. His tongue, slick and tender, toyed easily with her own. His hand slipped below her waist to draw her hips to his, making no secret of his physical wants beneath the fine linen of his trousers. His lips trailed along her jaw, his breath warm and eager in her ear a moment before dropping to tease the soft skin behind it.

A pleasant shiver ran through her, and she was vaguely aware that the footsteps she'd heard had stopped. A muted buzzer sounded and the door to the hotel clicked noisily before being opened and shut, admitting the guests who had stumbled upon this display.

I have to ask him in. What am I so afraid of?

As though reading her mind, Jacopo drew away to look her in the eye.

It was all right there, she thought; it was obvious he wanted her, and all she had to do was ask him to come to her room so they could be together. She focused her gaze just above the topmost button of his shirt, watched his Adam's apple bob there for a moment in the open "v," and took the leap.

"-Would you like-"

"-I have to go-"

They spoke at the same time, their sentiments canceling each other out.

Damn it, anyway.

She exhaled, aware that he was still holding her wonderfully close. Emily felt a new flush rise to her cheeks, squelching the rush of excitement from before.

"I'm sorry, Emily. I would like..." His words faded while he twirled a strand of her hair around his fingertips, seeming to admire it in the stairwell's dim light.

"I know, I know." Her disappointment was evident in her voice, but she didn't care.

"I have to be in Rovigo early, or else..." He shrugged, smoothing her hair over her shoulder with a gentle touch, and she gave a quick, staccato nod in response. "Emily?"

"Yeah?" She couldn't face him. Somehow, the tenderness in his voice made it worse.

His fingertips grazed her chin, then turned her face up toward his. She blinked crazily, partly to force back the nonsensical tears that threatened, partly because of the intensity of his gaze. The sense of exposure, of *nakedness* that she felt under his scrutiny made her tremble and she knew he could feel it.

Although she wanted to, desperately, she couldn't look away now. He was searching her eyes for something, or reading something there, already – which one it was, she had no idea. All she knew in that moment was that she wanted him to kiss her again, to come with her to her room and make love to her as many times as would be humanly possible before the sun came up.

A knowing quirk at the corners of his mouth gave her pause before he kissed her again, the tenderest, most gentle kiss he'd given her yet.

"*Buonanotte*, Emily," he said in parting, already turning to walk down the stairs and pressing the hotel's doorbell as he went.

"*Buonanotte*," she echoed, surprised to find her disappointment had faded. "Jacopo."

He stopped a few steps down from the landing, as the hotel door buzzed and the lock clicked open behind her.

"*Sì?*"

Emily shrugged and smiled.

"Nothing. I just wanted to say your name."

He smiled too, regarding her with easy warmth before he nodded and continued down the steps and around the corner, out of her view.

She turned to step into the hotel lobby, but as her hand touched the door, she heard his voice from the depths of the stairwell.

"Emily," was all he said, but the timbre of his voice was enough to give her another pleasant shiver before she stepped inside.

7

Jenn's eyes lit up with mischief as Emily entered the breakfast room the next morning. Emily glanced around, wondering who that smile was for, and upon seeing that Matteo was nowhere in sight, realized that it really was intended for her.

"So?" Jenn craned her neck to look around Emily before she sat down. "Where's your friend, this morning?"

"Um... Rovigo, I guess. Wherever that is."

"Rovigo?" Jenn wheedled, disappointed. "But you two were getting along so well, last night."

"So that was you in the hallway?"

"Yeah, Matteo and I got in pretty late. Not as late as some, though..." Jenn nudged Emily under the table with the toe of her shoe.

Emily shrugged and glanced around the room. "Where is Matteo, by the way?"

Jenn looked away, proof that she intended to evade the question.

"He had to go home. Never mind that, though. You're holding out. I want details."

Emily busied herself with pouring her tea, wondering just what there really was to say.

"To be honest," she said, stirring the sugar in and watching it dissolve, "I don't know what to tell you."

"Okay, I'll have mercy on you. Where did you meet?"

"At a paper shop. But I saw him the other night, on the Molo. I thought he was interested in you."

Jenn frowned at this last comment. "When did he ask you out?"

"He asked me to dinner when we left the shop."

"Um, hmmm..."

"I had him meet me here in the square. I didn't want to tell him which hotel I was in." Emily toyed with the edge of a napkin, flicking the crisp fabric between her fingertips.

"Better safe than sorry..." Jenn said with an air of impatience, gesturing for Emily to continue.

"Yeah. Anyway, he picked me up in his runabout, and took me to dinner at this place near the Rialto Bridge. It was really good, too. I mean, you know I don't like seafood or wine or stuff like that, but this was good."

"You drank wine? I had to twist your freakin' arm to get you to drink a Bellini!"

Emily nodded, abashed. "He's very persuasive."

"I'll bet." Jenn grinned and took a sip of her coffee. Her eyes fixed on Emily's face. "What then? Tell me the good stuff."

"Well, we went back to the bridge, and he kissed me." She couldn't resist either the blush or the smile which emerged with the memory. "We stayed there a while and then he said it was time to go. He brought me here, and..."

"...and?"

"He kissed me again; and it was... I don't know. It was so, I mean... It was different from the kiss on the bridge, you know?"

A rush of heat told her that her blush was deeper than ever.

Jenn leaned further over the table. "But did he come in with you? Didn't you...?" she whispered.

"No, he didn't." Emily shook her head, truly disappointed for the first time since Jacopo had gone. "We didn't."

Her friend sighed sympathetically. "I'm sorry to hear that."

"*You're* sorry?" Emily asked flippantly, surprising herself with a laugh.

Jenn laughed too. "I just thought, you know... I thought that you had done really, really well."

A soft smile touched Emily's lips before she took another sip of her tea.

"I *did* do really well. I did."

A few minutes passed in companionable silence.

"So, we're going to Murano, today, right?" Jenn asked, at last.

"That's right. I wanted to pick up something for Mom, and I've heard that some of the shops have nice jewelry, too. I just want something shiny and pretty, you know? A nice souvenir."

Jenn grinned as they stood up and walked to the front desk.

"What?" Emily asked, knowing her friend's smile meant something.

"I was just thinking – you could have had one heck of a souvenir, last night. From the way he was going, I really expected you to have a huge hickey this morning, at the very least."

Emily's laugh in response erupted more loudly than she'd anticipated, and she felt another rush of warmth to her cheeks. Jenn laughed, too, before they stepped up to the reception desk to turn in their keys.

"*Signorina*, this message arrived for you this morning." The clerk slid a small envelope across the counter to Emily. "Oh, and this package, as well." A small cardboard tube made a hollow *thunk* as the clerk put it on the marble countertop.

"*Grazie*." Emily took them and glanced over at Jenn before giving her friend a brief shrug. "Wait here; I'll be right back."

She left Jenn at reception and walked back to her room. Placing the cardboard tube on the bed, she sat down beside it. With trembling fingers she popped the wax seal of the small envelope and drew out the thick card-stock paper from inside. Unfolding it, she found neat, tight script, and a signature with a flourish that made her smile.

"Cara Emily,

I would like to offer to you this gift once again, and to extend an invitation to lunch this afternoon. Will you accept?

I will call this morning. If you will be out, please leave your answer at reception.

Yours,

Jacopo"

Emily stood and went to the window. Through the open curtains, she could just see the edge of the dock where he'd tied the runabout the night before. Unbidden, the memory of their kisses in the stairwell came to her and she allowed it to linger for a while. She fanned herself with the note, still smiling, and made her decision. After scribbling a swift, plain "Yes" onto a sheet of the hotel stationery, she hurried back to the front desk and gave the note and the key to the clerk.

"Let's go," she said, ignoring Jenn's questioning look. "We have a boat to catch, but I have to be back by lunchtime."

With Jenn's excited "Don't worry about me, I'll find ways to entertain myself!" still ringing in her ears, Emily made her way along the *calle* toward the hotel. Her friend's eager encouragement was reassuring, and Emily was relieved that Jenn didn't resent cutting short their excursion to the outer islands.

Jacopo was already outside the hotel when Emily arrived. He hadn't noticed her, so she ducked back around the corner to straighten her skirt and smooth her hair. The whole situation still had an unreal feel to it, she thought, examining herself in the reflection of a shop window.

I'm just waiting for the other shoe to drop, I suppose, but I'm going to enjoy this while I can.

She steeled herself and stepped out into the *campo* to stroll toward him with a confidence she was actually beginning to feel. All she had to do was remember the night before and the kisses they'd shared. It was enough to make her walk on air.

Jacopo's smile warmed an already sultry day, his hand surprisingly cool as he took hers and raised it to his lips for a soft air-kiss.

"You are lovely, Emily," he said, the words warm over her fingers.

"*Grazie*," she said. Her cheeks ached from the force of her smile.

He regarded her for a moment before shaking his head in an amused gesture. "*Non posso resistere...*" He chuckled before leaning in to swiftly plant a soft kiss on both cheeks.

Emily blushed anew, tingling where his lips had touched her.

Jacopo wrapped his arm around her waist and guided her along the *calle* to the dock behind the hotel.

"So, how was Rovigo?" she asked.

"*Niente di speciale*," he said, then noted the confusion on her face. "Nothing special. It was just work, and taking care of something for my mother."

"Oh."

"This reminds me of something. This afternoon, after our lunch, would it be okay if I stopped by my home? My mother is going to hospital, and I want to see her before she leaves." Jacopo held Emily's hand to assist her into the boat.

"Of course it's okay." Emily took a careful step off the dock and stood next to him in the boat. "I'm surprised you wanted to meet me, if your mother is ill."

"She has been ill a long time. This is just another trip of many, for her. Besides that," he said, "I want her to meet you."

Oh, my God.

"All right, then."

She sank down into the passenger seat before her legs could betray her. Only now it wasn't just being on the water that made her unsteady.

I've got to stop reading so much into this. I'll just go along for the ride and see where it takes me.

To her immense relief, he didn't ask any more blunt questions about her relationship status. That whole experience had been quite unsettling and provocative, and she didn't care to repeat it. Maybe that was simply how they did things, here, but she doubted that was the case.

He was trying to see if he could shock me. Who knows what the next salvo will bring?

Lunch was a modest affair, a sandwich and a coffee in a bar on a quiet square not far from the Grand Canal. Emily was pleased with how easily she'd managed to put her concerns behind her in order to relax and enjoy Jacopo's company.

He was a perfect example of someone utterly at home in his own skin. Emily watched closely, wondering how he did it. She noted his interactions with people along the walkways, in other boats when they were tooling along the canals, with the servers and the other patrons in the bar. The ease with which he moved in his environment was something she envied.

After lunch, they strolled across the *campo* toward the *rio* where he'd docked the runabout. A narrow bridge spanned the water, with a wrought-iron gate on the *campo* side and a huge arched wooden door on the other. The elaborate scrollwork of the iron in the gate revealed countless hours of work and a lifetime of training in every fine turn.

Emily longed to have her camera in her hands, to photograph the details of the ironwork.

"It's beautiful, isn't it?" she asked, trailing her hand along the spirals and twirls to feel the movement in the metal.

"*Sì*, it is. It is very old, too. At least one hundred years – but it has been treated well and does not rust, unlike others."

She turned to ask how he knew that for sure, but stopped upon seeing the large iron key in his hand. His gaze held hers as he stepped forward and slipped his key into the lock with a rather provocative gesture, a wicked grin on his face all the while.

Her throat went suddenly dry and she swallowed hard, a pleasant tingle sweeping through her body at the unspoken statement in his actions. The sound of the iron key in the lock had an audible heft to it, and she pictured the key pushing the tumblers about to unlock them.

While he closed the gate behind them, Emily's attentions drifted over the sides of the bridge, along the length of the *rio*. The day was quiet and peaceful in the midst of what Jacopo had called the "lunch rest."

Jacopo opened the wooden door at the far end to reveal a dilapidated courtyard beyond it. She stepped inside and, even in the open air, the wooden door closed with a dull thud that made the ground shake under her feet. The courtyard wasn't much to speak of. Sand-colored paving stones covered the ground, a few terracotta tubs holding stunted plants stood alongside the walls, which ended where a second wrought-iron gate – now padlocked shut – opened onto the *rio* itself. The walls of the palazzo were the same non-color as the paving stones, fading from sun-bleached white to pale beige just beneath the projection of the roof.

Every window was open. The shutters were locked back and lace curtains drifted in and out on the breezes. Jacopo led her to the single entrance, another wooden door set beneath a whitewashed archway. A stone winged lion curled along the top of the arch, his fierce, frozen features glaring down upon all who entered.

Emily paused, gazing up at this weathered sentry, a nervous smile playing across her lips.

"Do you like him?" Jacopo asked.

"I don't know. He's certainly interesting."

"He used to frighten me when I was a child. I'd play out here and sometimes I swear he'd move when I got too close to the gates."

Emily turned to face Jacopo and found him watching her. "Really? That would freak me out."

"It disturbed me as well, until my father explained that this was my protector. If I didn't go out of his sight, I'd be safe. Always." He chuckled to himself, shaking his head. "Of course, that meant not leaving the *cortile*, the courtyard. It took me a while to understand that was all he'd meant."

He opened the door of the palazzo and a brief rush of cool, musty air pushed past them. He stepped back and gestured into the darkness of the entryway. "Go to the right, and up the stairs," he said. "The left leads to the *rimessa*, below the house."

Which explains the smell, she thought.

The stairwell was dank and dimly lit, but every few steps upward brought fresher air and a bit more light. She reached a landing with windows at either end, sunlight filtering in through half-closed shutters to fall on chipped and cracked marble paving.

Jacopo drew out a more conventional key ring to unlock the rather unremarkable door. It opened onto a hallway, lined on the left with windows – the ones she'd seen from the courtyard, no doubt – and on the right by several doors, all of which stood open.

The door shut hard behind them, and a cool breeze swept through the windows toward the open doors. Jacopo paused for a moment, listening attentively.

"*Mamma? Sono io*," he called. "*Siamo qui.*"

"*Sono nella sala, tesoro*," came the frail response from the first room.

Jacopo took Emily's hand and led her into the room, where she struggled to avoid stopping short in wonder. The living room was large and airy, with exposed dark beams overhead and gleaming marble tiles on the floor. The walls glowed a soft, deep honey-gold. From the sofa and the guest chairs by the windows, to the *armadio* along the wall in the far corner, everything was clean and in pristine condition, though perhaps a bit worn by age. The carpet beneath her feet was faded from years of use, and to her untrained eyes it looked like an authentic, antique oriental rug.

His mother sat on a hardback chair next to a writing desk, facing the doorway as though in expectation of her visitors. Her thin, wizened frame seemed ready to blow away on the breezes sweeping through the room. She gave Emily an almost regal nod, and then gestured toward her son with scarcely hidden impatience.

When Emily's eyes adjusted to the light coming through the windows, she stifled a gasp, hoping that Jacopo and his mother wouldn't notice. The Grand Canal spread out in either direction, gleaming with metallic brilliance in the afternoon sun. She drifted to the windows, fighting her disbelief, while mother and son engaged in conversation.

"*Dai, Mamma...*" Jacopo's protest broke into Emily's contemplation of the view and she turned to face them, blushing.

How rude of me to just wander over here like that.

His mother smiled at her, a warm, open greeting. "*Ciao, Emilia. Come stai? Bella vista, no?*" She didn't seem the least bit troubled by Emily's wandering attention. If anything, she sounded pleased.

Jacopo grinned. "She says it's a beautiful view, no?"

"I-it is, indeed," Emily said, nodding her head and trying not to stammer.

"*Mamma, non si chiama 'Emilia.' Si chiama* 'Emmylee'. *È Americana.*"

The old woman shrugged her slumping shoulders in a gesture of utter indifference. "*Beh, fa lo stesso. È carina.*" She eyed him with a hint of disapproval. "*È piu carina delle altre donne con cui esci, ad ogni modo.*"

"*Sì, Mamma, è vero.*" Jacopo looked to Emily with an amused smile. "She says you're pretty. Prettier than my..." He paused uncomfortably for a moment and then continued. "Than my last girlfriends."

Emily smiled back, desperately wishing that she spoke Italian. She could see that this was no doddering old fool. This woman, despite whatever illness she might have, was sharp as a tack.

"*Prego; accomadati, tesoro.*" His mother gestured toward the sofa and Jacopo nodded encouragement.

Emily sat shakily, trying to appear more comfortable than she felt. "*Grazie, signora,*" she said, and received another cheery smile.

A bell rang, surprisingly loud in the empty corridor.

"*Ah, c'è Antonio,*" the old woman said with an air of satisfaction.

"*Scusa,* Emily. I must answer the door." Jacopo smiled and left the room.

"*Chi è?*" he asked, and a distant, metallic voice responded. "*Sì, okay; venite su,*" Jacopo answered in turn. Emily heard the *snick* of the door opening before he came back in. "*Sei pronta, Mamma?*"

"*Sì, sì...*" She waved one hand dismissively toward a single small suitcase by the door. "*Andiamo, finalmente.*" She glanced at Emily and smiled before facing her son once more. "*Jacopo, ricorda che cosa ti ho detto.*"

He nodded and then bent to place a kiss on her withered cheek.

"*Sì, Mamma, me ne ricorderò bene. Non potrei dimenticar me ne, non lo permetteresti.*"

It was clear from his tone that this was a conversation they'd had many times before, and he didn't welcome having it yet again. His mother barked out a short, amused laugh at this, and again Emily wished she had understood the exchange.

The curtains at the windows fluttered inward and the front door thumped shut. Two men entered the room, one pushing a wheelchair, the other with his faded and stained cloth cap in his hands. Their rough coveralls and stained t-shirts seemed out of place amongst the weathered elegance of the salon, but they were obviously familiar with their environs.

As one, they inclined their heads in a sort of bow, before Jacopo's mother reached out with shaky hands. The taller and thinner of the two, hat still in hand, bowed to allow her to plant a noisy kiss on his cheek. The other remained behind the chair, his fingers drumming on the grips, grinning all the while.

Murmured conversation followed, swift pleasantries of some sort, Emily guessed. Jacopo and the thin man moved to assist the elderly woman into the wheelchair. More conversation, then Jacopo's mother raised her hand in serene farewell to Emily before the two men wheeled her out of the salon and away.

"I will be back, Emily," Jacopo said, and went to the door. "Please make yourself comfortable."

He left without waiting for her to respond, and the front door closed solidly behind him once more.

8

Emily stood at the window, admiring the unexpected, magnificent view of the Grand Canal. From this vantage point, it lived up to all the expectations she'd had upon her arrival in Venice. Boats and *vaporetti* passed, filled with residents and tourists, deliveries and goods of all possible sorts, under the warm summer sun. She fancied she could smell the cooking in the restaurants nearby, or the overripe fruits and vegetables from the stands along the walkway below.

For a moment, she imagined she could smell the cocoa-butter sunscreen of the tourists baking themselves as they strolled past.

Oh, wait; that's me, isn't it?

The scent was subtle, but hers all the same. She turned to take a sly sniff of one bare shoulder and an instant later was surprised by Jacopo's hand on the other. Her attempt to suppress her startled jump failed, and he chuckled softly.

"Enjoying the view, *Cara?*"

She nodded then turned to face him, her heart leaping a little at the sight of him. He was so handsome, so golden, so...*leonine*, she thought, recalling the winged lion above the doorway of the palazzo. A perfect example of a Venetian gentleman, he even bore a resemblance to the city's emblem.

"'Cara'?" she asked.

"It means 'dear', as in precious," he explained, then laughed, adding, "or expensive."

"I'm expensive, then?" she asked with a smile, liking the play on words.

"Not in the least. Which is, of course something any man can appreciate."

Emily nodded and turned back to the window, unsure what to say to that. Instead, she changed the topic altogether.

"Your mother seems very sweet."

"Sweet? That might be overstating things." Jacopo's fingers grazed the skin of her arms, trailing up to her shoulders and down again, while Emily tried not to shiver at his touch. "She did seem to like you."

"Really? We barely met, and we couldn't understand each other."

"And yet *you* thought she was sweet."

"Fair enough."

"I'm glad you came. I didn't wish to choose between seeing either one of you, and I thought this was the best way."

Jacopo fell quiet, his fingers continuing their hypnotic tracing along Emily's bare arms. Her skin had goosefleshed under his touch, but he kept caressing the same line until she had no choice but to shiver and edge away before her whole body began to quiver.

Her knees went weak each time he touched her, and pleasant warmth seeped throughout her body from low in her belly as she drew away from him. He gave no indication, however, if he noticed anything odd in her behavior.

Emily settled in a chair near the window, delicately positioning herself on the ancient-looking pointelle fabric of the padded seat, fearful of damaging it. Jacopo moved to the window and opened the shutter further, catching a light breeze as it passed, affording her a chance to observe him in silence.

When he turned to her once more, she met his eyes and found them the color of the sky outside the window: a pale, barely-there blue. His golden skin seemed the same color as the walls of the palazzo, his hair the tawny blond of a lion's mane.

Making love to him would be like making love to Venice itself.

She shook her head to dispel the absurd – though appealing – thought.

"What is it, Emily?" he asked with a grin. The knowing tilt of his head led her to think that he knew all too well what she was thinking.

"Nothing."

Jacopo turned back to the window and leaned against the frame, his gaze steady on the canal and the travelers on it. His grin faded, replaced by a distant, almost vacant expression. The silence of the room seemed to absorb the sounds from outside as well. Dust motes dancing in a beam of light through another shuttered window moved to an unheard music.

Willing herself awake in the dozy quiet, Emily sat up straight. Jacopo left the window to slouch upon the antique sofa and study the marble floor at the edge of the rug beneath his feet. The ticking of the ornate clock on the far wall kept hypnotic time with Emily's heartbeat.

"My mother wishes me to marry," he said, his words echoing slightly in the grand room.

Even though she was sitting, Emily's knees went to water. Had she been standing, she would have hit the floor in a graceless slump. As it was, she found herself sliding back to sit in the armchair.

"Really?" she asked, hoping the delay wasn't noticeable.

"*Sì, è vero.*" Jacopo looked up at her at last. "That is; yes, it's true. She is fond of saying that she wishes for me to find a wife, before she dies. She wishes for me to be an honest man, with an honest woman." His expression was full of dark humor, a bitter turn to his mouth.

"Wow." At a loss for words, Emily wiped her suddenly clammy hands on her thighs, pulling the fabric of her skirt taut.

"This has become her favorite subject, with me: 'Find a wife, give me a grandchild.'" Jacopo's gaze drifted to the open window, focusing somewhere over Emily's left shoulder. "I can't believe it, but she said it again, just now when she was leaving."

"Just now?" She trembled, her pulse already racing. She drew a slow, deep breath, hoping Jacopo wouldn't notice. The light sweat along the back of her neck felt positively chilly, now.

What is he leading up to? It can't be, can it?

Jacopo blinked and his eyes shifted to her face, regarding her in silence before a short bark of laughter escaped him.

"*Oddio*! Emily! I didn't mean that she wants me to marry *you*."

Disappointment mingled with relief and Emily slumped into her chair, her energy drained. "I didn't think that," she said, the strength of her blush making her feel dizzy. "Honest."

Jacopo chuckled to himself, watching her for another moment from the sofa before he stood and crossed over to her. "Yes, you did," he said, nodding. "And it's my fault. My English isn't so perfect as I'd like it to be."

"Sorry." She turned in her chair to look over her shoulder out the window, until Jacopo's gentle touch on her cheek turned her to face him again.

He took her hands in his and simply stood before her, his eyes holding hers so that she didn't dare try to look away. Another warm breeze through the window carried the aroma of salt and damp on it, mingling with Jacopo's cologne and the scent of her sunscreen. The combination of smells mixed with the warmth of his hands holding hers made her tremble worse than before, as she sat looking up at him.

He knows what he does to me. He knows the effect he has on me, and it's not fair. I don't have any effect on him at all.

She forced herself to swallow, a dry effort in the damp air. He released one of her hands and reached to touch her hair, her cheek and chin, his fingertips lingering there while she blinked up at him, wondering what he wanted her for, why she was there.

The light pull on her hand drew her to her feet and then against him, so she could feel him breathing, his body warm and solid against her own.

Breathe, Emily. Breathe.

Underneath his cologne lay the clean scent of his skin and the salty tang of his sweat, both of them dancing enticingly at the back of her tongue. Remembering their first meeting, just the day before, she recalled having that same sensation. At once she wanted to close her eyes and smell him, but she was too afraid of how he'd react. Would he think it strange, or would he understand why she wanted to do that? She wasn't completely sure why, herself.

His arms slipped around her, slow and strong, holding her securely in place. She realized that if she wanted to pull away from him now, she wouldn't be able to. The knowledge both thrilled and frightened her. That low tremor in the depths of her told her she wanted more from him, regardless.

They were together, alone, in a palazzo on the Grand Canal, and no one else knew it.

Another thrill shivered through her, pleasant, tinged with apprehension. Then his lips were on hers, brushing gently, then tugging and parting them with casual, confident ease.

She returned the kiss, her arms winding around his neck as though of their own accord, and he held her to himself tighter than before. His kisses remained just out of reach; frustrating, enticing, forcing her to pursue him with ever more heated efforts.

Between each kiss she felt his smile, and soon she was smiling too. A delirious sort of happiness bubbled inside her and she sensed laughter squirming down deep, threatening to erupt at any moment.

She swallowed her laughter to drink him in, lapping at his lips and tongue with a strange, undefined thirst. His hands wound in her hair once more. He held her there with little effort, the gentleness of his touch belying his strength.

One of the shutters banged, startling them apart. Emily's knees wobbled beneath her while Jacopo went to fasten the shutter in place. He put his hands out on either side of the window frame and rested there. She watched him, well aware that her emotions were plain on her face, in her stance, and a sense of helplessness stole over her.

Just say it, anyway, she thought. *Tell him that you want him, right here and now. Don't let last night happen all over again.*

Her hand twitched, aching to blot away the moisture trickling down her back and into the front of her blouse, to press her clothes against the wetness on her skin to absorb it. Instead, she stood frozen to the spot, every tiny droplet tickling madly and without relief.

Jacopo remained at the window for what seemed like an eternity, his hair and skin haloing in the last of the late-afternoon light. At last, after one final glance toward the canal, he crossed to Emily and took her hand into his own.

Her heart leapt in anticipation.

"We should be going, now," he said. "You said you had to meet your friend for dinner, yes?"

"I do, but you know... it's really not that important. She'd understand if I didn't show up."

Jacopo nodded. "Perhaps. But that is the sort of thing she'd do to you, no?"

Emily sighed, knowing he was right. "I suppose so."

"Come, then."

He led her through the cool front corridor of the house and down the stairs to the ground floor landing. Her skin cooled fast in the dim light of dark passages where the air grew stale and changed little, and she shivered in spite of herself. The flashes of sunlight that bent along the floor and walls as they descended to the stone and concrete courtyard in front of the palazzo made a welcome break.

Before he opened the wooden door of the bridge, however, Jacopo paused. He gathered her into his arms and kissed her again with an unexpected, fervent passion that sent her mind reeling.

"*Allora, andiamo,*" he murmured a moment later, hefting the door open. "Let's go, then."

9

The door of her hotel room had barely closed before he kissed her. Emily sank into his embrace with a shiver of delight, returning his kisses in kind. She'd sensed his tension after leaving his home, but he'd said nothing to indicate what he thought, or how he felt.

Each kiss was hard and insistent, his lips pressing to hers with almost unseemly urgency. She saw no need to play coy or pretend that she wanted anything other than this, and was grateful for his sparing her the charade.

A memory of the interminable dance she'd done with Jason flickered through her mind. It had taken him months before he'd finally worked up his courage to take their kisses further. She pushed the remembrance aside, focusing on Jacopo; his kisses, his warm and spicy citrus scent, his hands caressing her breasts through the thin fabric of her blouse.

The late afternoon light filtered in through the shutters, casting warm bands of bright and dark across the room. She caught a glimpse of his eyes in that soft yellow light as he eased her down onto the bed, and a pleasant shudder slipped through her.

His kisses intensified and she drank them in, reaching to pull him closer only to feel him resist her touch. He pushed her blouse slowly upward, his fingers smoothing the fabric aside with an agonizing patience. She started a little at his tickling caresses but then held herself steady, savoring each slow gesture as it came.

His hand slid lower over her rounded belly to push down the waistband of her skirt. He paused and hesitantly retraced his fingers over the long indentation beneath her abdomen.

Emily winced, but forced her expression to become neutral once again before he met her eyes. She'd hoped he wouldn't notice, but it was useless to think that would happen. It was her bad luck, as it was. They always paused at the scar.

All the same, her panicked mantra echoed in her mind; *Please don't say it. Please don't ask, and don't say "I'm sorry," they always say that and they never mean it.*

Jacopo drew back to look, his eyes narrowed to focus in the dim light, his fingers tracing the scar from end to end. He met her eyes once again, clearly puzzled.

"Emily, is this...?"

She nodded. "It is."

"Why?"

"I was sick, once. Very sick. It was all they could do to help me." She laughed, a weak, defeated sound even to her own ears. "It seemed like a good idea at the time."

"When did this happen?"

She swallowed hard and gazed up at him. "I was seventeen. Almost eighteen, actually. I had, um… I had a..." She paused, drew a deep breath and plunged forward. Even as she said it, she heard the doctor's voice saying it with her, in the sympathetic tones he'd used when she was recovering. "…A miscarriage. It all happened so fast, I don't remember much. One minute I was at home in the worst pain I'd ever felt, the next, I was in the hospital being told I couldn't have —"

The twist of memory lodged in her throat, silencing her even as Jacopo's expression slowly faded to an unreadable blank. It was better than pity, though. It was also better than the cold, plain greed she'd seen in the few others, when they'd realized there was no chance she'd trap them.

Jason's face when he explained that he'd decided he wanted his own kids came to mind. She flinched away from the memory and found that Jacopo's fingers were still tracing the scar. His touch was light enough that she hadn't noticed. His gaze had fixed upon it, and Emily knew how it must look, shiny and faded pink against her pale skin, even in that warm light.

In time, he rested his palm over her abdomen and lay next to her without speaking. In her peripheral vision, she saw his brow knit with concern, then puzzlement before returning to that maddening blank expression.

She closed her eyes, not wanting to watch him anymore. She yearned to know his thoughts, but she remained silent. How could she ask? Did she really want to know what he was thinking?

To her surprise, he kissed her again. A tender, gentle parting of her lips, his tongue slipping between them. His hand left her abdomen and her skin cooled in the absence of his touch. His fingers twined in her hair, holding her in place, and she trembled beneath him.

It was like his kiss on the bridge the night before, all encompassing and canceling out everything else around her. There was only the two of them and the space they occupied. Nothing else mattered.

The taste of his kisses mingled with unshed tears at the back of her throat. She inhaled deeply when they parted, burying her face against his neck to take in the scent of his cologne and his skin. She licked her lips and savored the maleness and the smoothness of his skin beneath her hands, intoxicated by the adrenalin rush brought on by his touch.

His kisses trailed to her neck, his lips warm and firm, yet soft enough to tickle the sensitive flesh behind her ear. He cupped her breast with a gentle but insistent grasp, a hint of pressure behind the caress.

Emily reached for him, trying to pull him closer, but he evaded the effort and dropped his hand lower, instead. Once more his palm rested on her belly, the spread fingers of his hand nearly spanning the full width, and for the first time she felt small next to him.

His hand slipped lower still, and the thought vanished. His fingers eased beneath her skirt to curve over her in a delicate caress. They moved slowly, stroking her through her cotton panties, applying gentle pressure even as they spread to urge her thighs apart.

His tongue teased hers, moving in languorous strokes that seemed to echo the subtle dance of his fingertips. Emily trembled around his touch as his fingers pressed harder, seeking and finding what became the very center of her being. Her world shrank smaller and smaller until it ceased to be anything other than his touch upon her. Her hips rose to the rhythm he dictated, and she ached for the release it promised.

Her hand traced down his arm, past the fabric of his shirt at his shoulder and on to the warmth of his arm and the softness of the hair there. She stopped with her hand over his, her fingers spread over his in encouragement, urging him on.

"Like this…?" he murmured, his breath tickling her ear, and she nodded frantically when he followed her subtle lead. "Or this?"

The pressure increased in long, slow strokes that made her buck and curl beneath his touch, her hand flying to his shoulder once more.

"Like that, please; just like that…"

"Okay."

Then his mouth was hard upon hers, his fingers driving her swiftly mad. At last, she shuddered hard beneath him, her thighs clenching around his hand as she gasped in release. His manipulations didn't cease; he continued stroking until she came again, this time with a sharp, surprised cry.

Her throat was desperately dry, now. She wondered when it would be appropriate to get up and have a glass of water, and if she should offer one to him, as well. Or would that be some sort of strange breach of the mood?

Before she could ask, she reached for him and realized that he had moved away from her.

He stood and straightened his clothes, then went to the mirror beside the door to smooth down his hair, inspecting his reflection intently in the wavy glass.

"I'm sorry, Emily. I must go. I didn't realize it was so late," he said, and she thought the apology sounded quite sincere.

"Just like that?" She sat up to better face him.

He nodded. "I will see you again. Tomorrow morning?"

Sure you will.

She nodded her own response, swallowing down the sarcastic retort.

Jacopo crossed to the bed, knelt on it for a moment and kissed her as he had when they'd first arrived. For a moment, she hoped that he'd changed his mind and would stay after all, but he withdrew quickly and went to the door.

He lingered in the doorway for a few moments, his summer-sky gaze making her feel more exposed and vulnerable than she ever had.

A murmur of voices in the hall was silenced by the *snick* of the latch, leaving Emily alone in the quiet that followed.

I can't believe it. Two near misses in one day.

She sighed, trying not to listen for the engine of Jacopo's runabout. She didn't want to hear him go. Instead she wanted to cling to the delusion that he might return, knocking on her door, telling her "Never mind what I said before," and making love to her, straightaway.

It was maddening – positively maddening – that on two separate occasions within an hour of each other she had thought they were so close to consummating their relationship, only for everything to fall through.

Then again, from the looks of things, perhaps "relationship" was too big a word for what they had?

So what the hell is it, then?

She lay back, closed her eyes and folded her arms over them, fancying that she could still feel the fading warmth of his kisses and caresses on her skin. There was no denying the trembling of her legs or the final, quivering ache between her thighs. She wanted him so much it was actually painful.

Her frustration grew, and she wondered if it was unreasonable of her to feel the anger she did. Was he just toying with her, leading her to the brink and then abandoning her there on purpose? If so, why keep doing it?

For just a moment, she felt she'd as soon scratch his eyes out as make love to him.

Oh, right, that phrase again.

"Make love" seemed to imply something truer, something lasting – something far from the fling that this would be. That is, if it would happen in the first place.

Sitting up, Emily shook her head, trying to dispel the daze that threatened to settle upon her. The clock on the wall told her it was nearly seven, and almost time for dinner with Jenn. She ran her hand through her disheveled hair and stood to go into the bathroom. The cardboard tube Jacopo had left for her earlier caught her eye.

A half-smile touched her lips as she went to pick up the tube from the desk. Her hand rested atop it for a moment, a flicker of curiosity flaming out quickly in the back of her mind.

Never mind that for now. I'll open it later.

"So, you're saying that nothing's happened, yet?" Jenn's look of disbelief was nearly as wounding as the reality of the statement she'd made.

"No. Nothing at all. It's like we just manage to get to that point, and then..."

Jenn gasped. "You mean he can't...?" She made an obscene gesture just within Emily's sight, behind the table where they sat.

"I don't mean that!" Emily said with a groan. "It's just that we reach a certain point, and it's all going great, and then... Nothing. He stops or leaves."

"Oh, God. Is he married, do you think?"

"Definitely not."

"How can you be so sure? Why else would he skip the chance to... You know?"

Emily shrugged, uncertain. "I met his mother today."

Jenn's eyes popped wide, her mouth agape. "You did?"

"He took me to his house. She was leaving for the hospital when we got there. He said..."

"He said what?" Jenn stabbed at her plate of calamari, her attention momentarily focused on spearing a piece of squid.

"His mother wants him to get married. Soon."

A forkful of pasta and calamari slipped off the side of Jenn's plate.

"He told you this?"

Emily nodded. "No big deal, though. He told me she didn't mean for him to marry me."

"He actually said that?"

"Yes, he did." Emily slouched in her chair and sighed. "It's not a big deal, really. I guess maybe he's kinda freaked out by the whole situation. Maybe that's why he backs off at the last minute."

"All I can say, Mouse, is... Well, I'm sorry. I really thought this would be it for you, you know?"

"So did I, Sissy. So did I."

10

"So," Emily said, minding the walkway as it narrowed and followed the contour of a palazzo, veering away from the main canal, "what exactly happened to Matteo? You never did tell me."

"He had to go home. That's all." Jenn fidgeted, her fingers tapping the side of her tiny purse. "Okay. He had to go home to his wife."

"His wife?" Emily stopped short and Jenn turned to face her, a light flush in her cheeks.

"That's right, his wife. I know, shocking, isn't it?"

"Yeah, it is." Emily resumed walking. "I mean, you know... Wow." She resisted pull at the corners of her mouth, determined to keep a straight face. "I didn't think he was old enough to be *married*."

Jenn stared at Emily until she could no longer hold back her laughter.

"Fair enough," Jenn sniffed. "He *was* a bit young, even for us."

"Even for *you*, that is." Emily held her head high. "At least I picked an older man."

Jenn snorted a laugh of her own and Emily followed suit as they made their way back toward the hotel.

"God, can you believe this heat?" Jenn asked with a sigh, fanning herself with one hand. "It's not as bad as earlier, but the air conditioning is so weak in my room, I hope I'll be able to sleep tonight."

"You'll be fine. It's only a couple of nights more, right?"

"Yeah." Jenn paused, longing in her eyes as a couple passed them by.

"What's the matter?"

"Ice cream."

"What?"

Jenn turned to her, a slow smile spreading across her lips. "Did you see the ice cream cones those two had?"

Emily grinned. "I did. Too bad we had so much for dinner."

Jenn took Emily's hand and pulled her along in the direction the couple had come from.

"Don't be ridiculous, you ate like a bird," she scolded. "I want ice cream."

"They call it *gelato* here, remember? It's not the same thing."

"It's better, and I want it. Come on, Mouse. Let's indulge. Besides, when we get home, the good times will have to end."

The *gelateria*'s storefront lit the entire street in a soft neon glow, and the benches propping the doors open allowed artificially-cooled air to seep enticingly outward. Emily shivered when they entered, her eyes widening at the colorful display in oblong stainless-steel bins that filled the refrigerated cases. Dozens of frosted tubs of bright colors were lined up inside, the flavors they contained written in Italian or what Emily guessed was the local dialect.

She thought of Jacopo, speaking with the man in the restaurant in an utterly incomprehensible and somehow still *more* foreign tongue. The recollection brought with it both a hint of warmth and pull of longing for him.

Jenn debated her choices for an embarrassingly long time. Emily ordered by pointing out her selections and fumbling through her pronunciations of their names. The server was curt without being rude, and Emily was certain that, were Jenn not there being, well, *Jenn*, his patience would have run out much faster. When more patrons entered and Jenn still hadn't decided, the server simply took his spatula in hand, slathered some random selections precariously onto a cone and thrust it into her hand, waving her off.

"I got a freebie," Jenn said as they turned to go out of the shop. Her expression was childlike, full of surprise and delight.

Emily rolled her eyes in playful disbelief then carefully sampled her own delicately-balanced heap of gelato, unable to prevent the satisfied hum of pleasure that escaped her. She sat on one of the empty benches and Jenn settled beside her.

"How good is this?" Emily asked. "I got pistachio, rice and chocolate. What did you get?"

"Hmmm... I got..." Jenn licked daintily at different spots on the cone, her tongue flicking and darting artfully from flavor to flavor. Emily couldn't help noticing several men had paused in the doorway while enjoying their own treats, to observe her. "I got... I don't know. There's coconut, and this is sort of vanilla... this last one is chocolaty, but there's something more to it. It sure melts fast." She giggled, then closed her eyes to lick at a rivulet dripping down the cone toward her hand. "God, it's so rich, though... Mmmm..."

Emily looked away, embarrassed by the obvious attention the men were giving Jenn, now, and tried to focus on her cone.

"Yeah," Jenn continued, "there's something like hazelnut or whatever in there."

"Nutella?" Emily offered, blushing and hoping the artificial light would hide it.

"No, it's deeper, it's more like, like —"

"*Gianduia*," a new voice offered.

Emily turned slowly back toward the group outside the shop, toward that oh-so-familiar voice.

Jacopo nodded in Jenn's direction and Emily watched her best friend hesitate before taking another long, lingering taste.

Does she even know she does it?

"*Gianduia*," Jenn echoed, her pronunciation almost a purr. "That's what it is."

Emily shook her head, then turned her attention back to Jacopo. He met Jenn's eyes steadily. There wasn't even a hint of flirtation in Jacopo's face, nothing to indicate any interest at all, unlike those of the other men milling around in the street.

His eyes flicked toward Emily and then back to Jenn once more.

"You must be Jenn," he said, and Jenn's eyes widened with incomprehension even as her lips made little peaks and rills in her gelato. "I am Emily's...friend, Jacopo." He extended his hand and Jenn took it stiffly, still thrown.

Jacopo gave her hand a formal, almost businesslike shake before releasing her.

"Emily," he said, and Emily shivered pleasantly. He'd said her name just as he had the night before in the stairwell, when he left.

The intonation was full of promise; she had no doubt about that.

"Jacopo." She smiled up at him, aware that Jenn was gaping at her in disbelief.

He smiled back.

"Jenn," he said, his voice gentle and warm as the surrounding night air, "would you mind if I speak with your friend? I have some apologies to make."

"By all means," Jenn said, coming back to herself at last. She gave Emily an encouraging look. "Please do."

"*Grazie*," Jacopo said, offering his hand to Emily, now. "Come," he said and folded her hand into his own before bringing her to her feet.

She had just enough time to glance over her shoulder and get a thumbs-up from her friend before Jacopo led her around a corner and down another street to a deserted *campo*. There, he stopped and reached for her other hand and Emily realized that she still held her melting cone of gelato.

"Oh, shoot." She held her hand away from herself, checking to be sure she hadn't dripped onto her clothes, then looked up to find Jacopo's broad, amused grin.

Without a word, he took the soggy cone and tossed it into a corner of the *campo* before she could protest. His eyes on hers all the while, he took her hand in his, carefully raised it to his lips and kissed away the trails of sticky-sweetness.

The warmth of his lips moving smoothly over her skin made her tremble, just like always, but she didn't care if he noticed. She was determined to tell him that she wanted to be with him before she left Venice, to ask if he felt the same way, and why did he keep stopping, in the end?

The look in his eyes stayed her tongue. The words piled up, unspoken.

In the silence of the dimly lit *campo*, she heard only the sound of their breathing, a low undercurrent accompanying the cool breeze that wove through the warmth of the night.

Kiss me, she thought. Kiss me, and I'll show you what I'm thinking, okay?

Their gazes remained locked until he released one hand and led her by the other along the unfamiliar *calli*, choosing turns in a seemingly random manner. She gave up on keeping track of where they were. Her heart thumped hard both from the pace of their walk and her growing certainty of where they were going.

Jacopo strode with blind confidence along the canals, leading them through wide *campi* and piazzas filled with light to dark alleys too narrow for them to walk side by side, across bridges and through archways large and small. They passed markets closing for business and restaurants opening for late dinner service, and he hardly spared a glance in any direction other than straight ahead.

It's like a tour of the city on fast-forward.

When he pulled up short Emily tried not to be obvious about drawing deep, grateful gasps of humid air while he fumbled in his pocket for something. Her knees trembled for a moment when she recognized the wrought-iron gate and the walkway over the *rio* before them.

The heavy iron sound of the key in the lock drew her back to the present once more. He swung the door open and stood aside, gesturing for her to precede him onto the wooden plank bridge. She did and he closed the gate with a strong shove. The metal grated in protest before clanging closed with an eerily final sound. The noise of the gate seemed too loud in the darkness and Emily winced. Jacopo touched her shoulder and guided her along to the end of the walkway.

He unlocked the wooden door in the stone wall. It took a little more effort to push this one open. He paused to wait for her to step into the courtyard before he shut the door behind them with another forceful effort.

"Emily."

She faced him, surprised. It was the first time he'd spoken since leading her away from Jenn and the *gelateria*. His voice sounded husky in the darkness and Emily shivered in spite of the evening's warmth.

There was no direct light where they stood, and her eyes were slow to make out the expression on his face. In the ambient light, his leonine features seemed made of sandstone, his hair bone-white. His hands were warm when he pressed them to her cheeks, framing her face in his velvety touch. She sought his eyes but couldn't quite discern the emotion within them in the dim light.

His lips pressed against hers in a slow caress, parting them with a subtle insistence. The soft pull of his lips made her shiver again, before the answering pull deep inside her swelled to a throbbing ache between her thighs.

It's all too easy for him, isn't it? I won't be able to stand it if we don't see things through again.

She reached for him and he drew her closer still. One hand at the small of her back held her against him while the other stroked her hair. Kissing her all the while, he traced his fingers down her side and back up again, then cupped her breast through the fabric of her blouse in a startling, possessive movement.

Emily drew away with a small gasp before he pulled her back to kiss her again, harder this time, his tongue in ardent pursuit of her own. She returned the kiss in kind, deepening it when he guided her to wrap her arms around his neck and press herself to him.

His hands were seeking again, slipping under her blouse to stroke her breast through her bra. His thumb traced over her nipple in maddening circles while she shuddered helplessly beneath his fingers, unable to pull away to lessen the intensity of his touch.

He ended their kiss and brought his lips to her throat, his tongue flicking and trailing along her flushed skin. Over his shoulder, Emily caught a glimpse of the canal through the archway, lights from the *campo* glinting over the surface of the water while an oar splashed in a distant rhythm, coming closer.

Jacopo's hand dipped lower still, gathering her skirt up in his fingers before darting beneath the loose fabric to grasp at her hip and hold her in place. He moved against her, a low, urgent sound escaping the depths of his throat, and she quivered anxiously in response even before he slipped his hand between her thighs to stroke her as he had that afternoon in her hotel room.

She gasped again, in part for the caress itself, but also for the ease with which he found the precise spot he needed to make her shiver uncontrollably and seek more of his touch.

This time, his finger curled around the edge of her panties, slow and insinuating, going deeper than before. He toyed with her until she buried her face against his shoulder, shuddering and ready to weep with need. He slid first one finger inside her, then two, stroking slowly, and her hips moved of their own accord, seeking more of his touch.

She swallowed part of her cry, muffling the rest against him while she gave in to his caresses, her body arching to his, her hips bearing down upon his hand in trembling, shaking acquiescence.

He continued kissing her throat and neck, lips and teeth nipping at her skin while she struggled to regain some sort of control over herself. She realized that she was clinging to him, now, fearful of losing her footing if forced to stand on her own.

It's just not possible. This is what I've read about in books, but it doesn't really happen, does it?

There was no time to ponder the question. He pulled her arms away from his neck and released her, moving a few paces away to regard her in the absolute and eerie silence of the courtyard.

Emily bit her lip, hard, and tried to ignore the pain in her already tender skin.

I'm going to scream, I swear. What did I do wrong? Why does he have to stop now?

"*Vieni con me.*" Jacopo seized her hand and pulled her along behind him, rushing to the door of the palazzo. She followed blindly, blushing furiously as relief flooded her body with adrenalin.

Perhaps there was hope, after all.

11

I t all passed in a whirl: the lion over the archway, the musty stairs
leading up the chilly stairwell to the upper floors, even the plain
front door which Jacopo heaved open and closed with a show
of impatience. Emily clutched his hand in hers, focusing on his
warmth in the darkness, her excitement warring with anxiety as
Jacopo switched on the light in the foyer. He led her through the
long corridor with the open windows, taking her past the grand
sitting room and into unknown territory.

Now they stood in a room she hadn't seen on her visit earlier that
day. The light from the foyer barely reached the doorway. Most of
the illumination came from the windows, reflecting off the pale walls
to give the room a hazy, unfocused glow. Heavy brocade curtains
framed the windows; an aged Oriental carpet lay atop the shining
marble floor, and an ornate wrought-iron bed frame draped with
luxurious silk bedcovers stood against the wall, a gauzy canopy over
the head of the bed shifting ghostlike in a scarcely-felt breeze.

Jacopo's bedroom resembled a museum display rather than a
place to rest.

Emily licked her dry lips as butterflies flitted in her stomach.
Jacopo stood close behind, though not touching her. Her breathing
grew shallow. It seemed a very real possibility that she might faint
dead away on the spot if she didn't pull herself together.

It's too perfect. Something has to go wrong, soon.

She startled under Jacopo's hand when he touched her hair; almost at the same instant, he withdrew his touch with a sharp intake of breath. Whirling around to face him, she was surprised to find him looking at his hand and chuckling softly.

"What's funny?" she asked, overcome by a sinking sensation. Was it all a joke, then?

"Didn't you feel it?"

"Feel what?"

Jacopo raised his hand and laughed. "We made a sparkle, when I touched you."

"A what?" She frowned, trying to understand what he'd meant.

"A sparkle. Like electricity."

"Oh." She smiled, understanding, and found herself slowly calming. "A spark? Really?"

"*Sì*, a spark. That's never before happened to me."

"Me neither." Her smile broadened.

So that was a first for both of us, then.

Jacopo's expression grew serious. He reached for her and she went to him, hesitating when his hand grazed her skin. Their eyes met and she shrugged.

"I suppose it was a one-time thing," she said, uncertain but trying to hide her disappointment.

"Perhaps. But let's keep trying."

They kissed with a slow care that she found distracting at first. Where had the passion from before gone?

Jacopo pulled her closer, his hands lingering where her waist curved into her hips, rubbing his palms in smooth, warm circles. She wrapped her arms around his neck, savoring the sensation of him, so warm and so solid in her embrace, the scent of his skin tantalizing beneath his cologne.

Almost of their own accord, her lips parted and she touched the tip of her tongue to his throat, sliding it up and over his Adam's apple to taste the salty earthiness of him. The rumble from deep in his throat served as response enough for her.

He clutched her to him, kissing her hungrily as though she'd been denying him all along, and not the other way around. He ground his hips against hers, his need for her evident and unabated. Emily felt that familiar weakness once more, coupled with her own desperate ache.

She clung to him while he led her closer to his bed, his fingers fumbling with the buttons of her blouse before he pushed her away to wrest the garment impatiently over her head. The blouse landed somewhere near the corner of the room, the buttons clattering on the marble floor. Impatient to feel his hands on her skin, she reached to undo her bra but he stopped her. Jacopo's touch had none of the desperate fumbling she was accustomed to; his fingers unfastened the clasps with a single deft motion before a flurry of caresses and kisses found her bared flesh.

A shiver threaded through her body, a thrill of excitement that he was truly going to make love to her, this time.

She twined her fingers in his hair, feeling the blond waves tangle and smooth out under her touch. Her heart raced until she feared it could burst. The sight of his lips and tongue working the sensitive skin of her nipples was overwhelming. She closed her eyes to focus on his kisses as he explored her. No-one in her past had ever given her this much attention, no-one had made her feel almost drunk and delirious simply by touching her this way.

Is it like this for everyone else? Is this why Jenn is so obsessed with sex?

Jacopo's fingers fairly flew down the front of his own shirt, preventing her from attempting to unfasten them herself. Denied that pleasure, her fingertips twitched with a desire to touch him, to feel his skin against her own.

When he held her to him once more his skin was surprisingly hot, and she wrapped her arms around him to keep him close. She felt his pulse against her lips when she kissed his throat, and the throb between her thighs ached in sweet accompaniment. He tightened his arms around her so her breasts pressed to his chest and his golden curls there brushed against her erect nipples. Her head swam with a delightful dizziness while her skin tingled.

She hadn't noticed that he'd backed them all the way to the bed until she fell onto the mattress, still clinging to Jacopo as though life itself depended on it. The weight of him atop her only intensified the drunken feeling and she fought the urge to laugh out loud for fear that it would destroy the moment.

Who laughs during sex, anyway? What the hell is wrong with me?

With patient effort, Jacopo slowly peeled her arms away and moved further from her. She stilled anxiously – surely he wouldn't stop now?

A quiet chuckle escaped him and he slipped one hand underneath the waistbands of her skirt and panties to draw them slowly down her hips. She trembled in time to her heartbeat, certain he could feel it where his hand rested on her, his eyes seeking hers in the half-light.

And that's that. Now he's seen me naked, he'll lose interest, right?

Instead, he kissed her again, his hand straying lower still, caressing in slow, tight circles. He found her as easily as he had before, and she shuddered against his hand with a gasp and soft sound of delight. His caresses continued until she shook uncontrollably, the pleasure becoming painful even as she sought more of the same. She rolled her hips toward him, anticipating his touch and the fact that she would repeat this movement as long as it took to feel fulfilled.

Blessedly, it didn't take too long.

Thankful for the darkness and the low illumination through the windows, Emily was too aware of the flush that heated her skin even as she calmed. Heat radiated from her body, inescapable in the night air, and the bedclothes clung, already damp, to her back. The stillness of the evening brought no relief through the open windows. Jacopo's nearness was intoxicating, his scent heavy around them, mixing with her own where it remained on his fingers.

"*Come una donna di Botticelli,*" he murmured against her skin, trailing his lips over her in sweeping circles, arcing ever upward. He lingered over her breasts, pausing to tease first one nipple, then the other, making her shiver yet again, raising gooseflesh in spite of the warmth of the room.

He took her hand in his and placed her palm against his body, then moved beneath her touch, letting her feel for herself the hardness of his arousal through his trousers. The yearning flooded into her again, sudden and all-encompassing as though poured down from a great height.

A small whimper escaped her throat and she realized she couldn't speak. She swallowed hard, stunned to find that she was salivating at the thought of touching him, feeling him inside her, and a flush of mortification swept over her body.

This is pathetic – my God, has he really reduced me to this?

Jacopo slid out from under her touch and she resisted the urge to grasp him back to her. He stood beside the bed and unfastened his belt and trousers with an apparent, practiced calm, then remained there, giving no sign that he would join her. She quaked with impatience, silently willing him to rejoin her.

Even in the semi-darkness, his gaze was intense and she was his sole focus.

It was both pleasing and intimidating.

Grateful for the shadows hiding her face, Emily allowed her own gaze to slip over him, drinking in the sight of his naked form. She struggled to control her breathing while the sense of unreality came over her. With effort she pulled her gaze away from his erection, up over the taut muscles of his abdomen and back to his eyes, which remained focused intently upon her. He took another step closer but still didn't join her on the bed.

Even now, in the ambient light through the windows, he was still pale gold from head to toe. This close, she could smell his subtle, earthy musk. Her tongue passed over her lips and she yearned to taste all of him, to lose herself in the salty velvet of his skin, the mineral richness that was uniquely his.

He smiled down at her, one eyebrow arching in a sly gesture which suggested he knew her thoughts. It was maddening, the way he always seemed to anticipate her desires. She knew his obvious confidence was part of what made him so appealing. She was also sure that she was just another conquest for him – and for the moment, she didn't really care.

With a tilt of his head he indicated that she should shift position on the bed, and she did so, watching him all the while. He reached to open the drawer of the nightstand and she heard the telltale rustle of an open box and the crinkle of foil as his long fingers sought something.

Just beneath her fluttering heart, her relief was a cool spot in her chest as she realized how unprepared she'd actually been for this moment.

As he approached her at last, an absurd image of a large, tawny lion stalking toward her flashed through her mind. She couldn't stop the chirp of a giggle that erupted from her, shaking her with a gentle tremor. Jacopo paused and Emily searched his face, desperate to let him know she hadn't meant that laugh for him at all. To her delight, he was smiling too.

"I–" she began, and he stopped her at once, his mouth hard upon her own, his lips parting hers so all she could do was give in and give way. It was easy enough to do. Coherent thought fell to the wayside in short order, leaving her to interpret her world in a more primal way.

Jacopo's kisses were passionate and fierce, those of a lover denied for ages, not what she expected of a fanciful fling or a one-night-stand. It was a struggle to keep up with him, to return the kisses with fervor equal to what he stirred within her.

Emily grasped at him, her hands shaking, her whole body thrumming as she yearned to have all of him at once. She wanted to wrap herself around him, take him in, touch and taste and watch him all at the same time. The impossibility of it was monumentally frustrating.

She struggled not to lose control too soon, not to give in and become frantic in her efforts. She wanted to make this last for more than a few manic moments. Occasional pleas from the depths of her brain urged her to focus, to savor the moment and commit it to memory, but she plunged headlong into every sensation, abandoning each one for the next as it came.

His caresses slid between them, lower and lower still, until the soft sounds of her excitement no longer seemed intrusive in the night air. She shivered beneath his touch, yearning to press her thighs together to still the pulse beating under his fingertips, which were poised over the too-sensitive flesh. He held himself back and she raised her hips to his, attempting to entice him.

Instead he remained as he was, suspended over her, just out of reach, teasingly close but giving her no satisfaction. She tried to grasp his hips to draw him closer, but he evaded her with an uncanny ease.

Her jaw clenched but the sound of her frustration still edged past her lips. She was close to tears, the frantic energy winning in spite of her best efforts to stop it. Words she'd never dreamed of saying in her life battled to slip past her reserve – she longed to beg him to fuck her, fuck her and never stop, just stop waiting and stop torturing her this way. She continued to fight the urge until at last she opened her eyes and met his heavy-lidded gaze.

"Jacopo, please–"

That was all it took. Emily exhaled a long, grateful sigh as he eased into her, filling her as his weight sank them both into the mattress. Their shared warmth wrapped around them like the night closing in. She spread her shaking hands over his back to feel his muscles flex as he moved inside her.

Her body responded to his in a way she didn't recognize, writhing and straining to meet his every movement, matching his every gesture. She quivered around him, aware that she was perilously close to coming.

Equally foreign was the sound of her voice, rising to an urgent, impassioned cry. She craned her neck so she could touch her lips to the hollow of his throat and mute herself. Without warning, Jacopo pushed her back, swept her legs up and anchored them with his arms, then thrust harder, quickening to a frenzy.

She tangled her hands in the sheets, seeking purchase to keep from sliding back with the force of his efforts. It was almost impossible to reciprocate from this position. The telltale hesitation in Jacopo's hips told her that he was nearing his own finish.

The scowl that twisted his handsome face assured her she was correct, even before his harsh "*Vengo!*" was growled in her ear.

His thrusting stuttered when he swelled within her, surprising her with the strength of his climax and spurring her closer to her own. She closed her eyes to savor the sensation and lost herself in it, delighted that he could continue for so long after he'd finished.

It wasn't until she'd exhaled a slow, shaky breath and relaxed around him that Jacopo stopped at last. He eased her legs to rest on either side of him, his touch a gentle contrast to his manner just moments before, and propped himself up on his forearms without speaking.

Emily opened her eyes to find him gazing down at her, silent. He brushed her hair back from her face with that same caring touch, and she felt her breath hitch at the expression in his eyes. The tenderness she saw there was both unexpected and touching. Her eyes held his, and for once it seemed as though he couldn't look away.

Her heart thudded once, twice, hard enough to shake her entire body. She blinked and Jacopo's tender expression was gone, the familiar blank mask of deep thought in its place.

He licked his lips before giving her a slow, deep kiss, and the tingling she felt over her whole body refocused.

"*Ti è piaciuto, amore?*" he murmured.

She blinked in response. "What?"

His brow furrowed, his eyes narrowing until understanding lit within them. "I mean to ask: you are satisfied?"

"Yes, indeed." Emily's face felt as though it was sparkling with the blood which rushed into her cheeks. "But do you really need to ask? It's not obvious?"

"I prefer to hear it from you, *amore*."

"I thought you already had," she said, and he laughed against the curve of her neck, tickling her.

He lingered with her for some time, giving her gentle kisses and touching her face lightly with his fingertips while she dozed and savored his weight atop her. She felt him going slowly soft inside her. A moment later, he withdrew from her and lay by her side.

Emily turned to watch him, the silence of the room broken only by their breathing and the ticking of the grandfather clock in the hallway. Jacopo stretched beside her, the ambient light grazing his skin and casting shadows that accented the contours of his body. He put his hands behind his head, affording her an even better view and when he smiled, she knew that he'd done it just for her.

A logy sense of satisfaction wrapped around her, and she smiled, half-wishing she were already telling Jenn every little detail. Her eyelids were suddenly heavy, the rush of energy ebbing as swiftly as it had arrived and leaving her limbs leaden. If he asked, she wouldn't be able to lift her head from the pillow, nor her arms and legs from the tangle of the sheets.

The sound of Jacopo removing the condom made her open her eyes, though only just enough to see him padding around the foot of the bed. He moved out of the room and down the hallway, and Emily struggled to keep her eyes open, to no avail. The distant rush of water in the bidet faded out into nothingness, and she slept.

12

The light was different. Emily was certain that the colors dancing behind her closed eyelids were different, too.

She peeked through her lashes, and found the world alight in shades of blue. The crimson and gold bedclothes, rumpled as though they'd been slept on, but not under, stretched out to the black wrought-iron bed frame. On the silken surface a vague outline of a body was still discernable amidst the disarray.

But who –?

With almost physical force, Emily's memory of the previous night clarified. She flinched ever-so-slightly before noting something else: she was lying on her side with one leg drawn upward, her other leg straight along the length of the bed.

This was not her usual rigid and anxious repose, not at all. She had never woken up in a relaxed position like this in a bed that wasn't her own. Certainly not after having made love to someone, anyway.

Where is Jacopo?

Her sleep-weighted eyes adjusted slowly. Still peering through her lashes, she spied Jacopo sitting in the wing chair next to one of the windows. In spite of the faint chill of the early morning he was nude, and a pleasant tremor shook her as she regarded his body from a distance. His hair was in tousled disarray, and her fingers tingled with a desire to stroke it into place again. His gaze fixed upon some midpoint between himself and the bed, but his face appeared utterly without expression.

A small shiver ran through her from head to toe, followed by a prickling of her skin so intense it pulled at the sheets under her.

The sheer curtains shifted in the breeze pushing through the open shutters. A stronger gust followed, flipping the edge of one panel up to obscure Jacopo from her vision, and she closed her eyes while the fine hairs of her arms raised as if someone had walked over her grave.

Emily pictured the winged lion over the doorway in the courtyard, his frozen snarl preferable to the vacancy in Jacopo's face. Several minutes passed while she waited for Jacopo to join her. She then realized it was doubtful he would.

The breeze grew warmer on her skin while the light behind her eyelids turned a dusky rose color. The sun was coming up. She'd spent the night with him.

If this is what I wanted, then why am I not happy about it? So he's in deep thought over there. So what?

The feeling wasn't right. There was more to it, but she didn't want to dwell on the negativity. Better to focus on happier thoughts, to recall the night before with clarity before the memories could slip away.

She blinked her eyes open to squint against the sunlight reflecting through the window. The coolness of the air on her skin reassured her that the hour was still early, but the sun was higher than she expected to find it.

How long have I been out this time?

Jacopo wasn't there. Emily shifted position, ignoring the dampness in the small of her back where the bedclothes clung to her. She yawned and stretched, her hand grazing the cool metalwork of the headboard before she curled up again. Her gaze swept over the bedclothes and back to the headboard once more. Tentatively, she reached up to trace her fingers over the spirals and turns of the metal where sinuous vines in elegant tangles wrapped themselves around quatrefoils that brought the city's architecture to mind.

She imagined silken scarves looped through the swirls, trailing down onto the pillows before her vision went blank, as though obscured by a silken smoothness of its own. Her legs tangled in the sheets until he flung the bed linens onto the floor, creating a soft breeze that cooled her body. She felt his hands at her wrists, securing her with the scarves, his musk filling her lungs before he drew away. She acquiesced completely, resisting nothing, wanting more.

Gasping at the sudden intensity of the sensations, she opened her eyes to the gauzy canopy overhead. The corners of it twined around the bedposts and descended to puddle on the floor by the headboard, drifting back and forth in the warming breeze on the way. The gentle movement lulled her toward sleep once more.

The sound of footfalls padding along the marble floor disrupted her doze. Jacopo stood at the foot of the bed, clad in a plush, golden yellow cotton bathrobe. He toweled his head with the hood, watching her.

Emily sat up, pulling at the bedclothes in an instinctive move to cover herself. Just as quickly, Jacopo knelt on the bed to place his hands over hers, halting her with a commanding gesture. She stilled beneath his touch and he gave a single shake of his head before he stood and resumed his place and his watchful gaze.

She met his gaze as best she could, aware if she looked around the way she longed to, her darting eyes would seem frantic, panicked. It took all her will to face his appraisal without blushing or curling up into herself. All the same, her mouth dried and her stomach threatened a nervous rumble to break the silence.

"When are you leaving?" Jacopo asked.

"Um, what?" Her spirits sank at the implication behind his words, her fingers twining in the sheets until it hurt. This was what she'd feared all along, what it always came down to. She exhaled slowly in anticipation.

All good things come to an end, right?

"When are you leaving?" he repeated. "Venezia, I mean."

"Oh," she said, a smile of relief tugging at her lips. "Tomorrow morning. Jenn and I are taking a water taxi from the station to the airport, I think."

The familiar blankness washed over Jacopo's face. Emily studied him from her position on the bed, too shy to move and disturb his contemplation. He seemed to have forgotten that she was there at all.

Jacopo's eyes narrowed, his brow knitting until a small crease formed over the bridge of his nose. He leaned against the bedpost and one hand rose to cover his mouth while his gaze strayed out the window toward the palazzo on the opposite side of the canal. He raised his head and trailed his fingers over his pursed lips before his eyes focused and flicked back to Emily.

"What if you didn't go tomorrow?" he asked from behind his fingers. "What if you stayed here longer?"

Oh, my God...

This beautiful man was actually asking her to stay in Venice. He wanted to spend more time with her. It was impossible, but she couldn't pinch herself to see if she was dreaming again without drawing his attention to it.

"I can't do that," she said at last, her insides doing a heavy, slow roll. "As much as I'd love to, I just can't."

"Why not?" he asked, and his face filled with genuine surprise. The downturn of the corners of his mouth in a disappointed frown threw her.

Emily's hand rose to suppress the sudden ache beneath her breast.

"Work and school, mostly. Then there's my mother, who would probably fly over here to get me herself. Not because she misses me, though – she'd hate to know I was having such a good time." Emily forced a small chuckle, her eyes on him all the while. When Jacopo smiled, a distinct relief lessened the tightness around her heart.

"I see," he said, his tone thoughtful. "I'd take care of this."

Emily appreciated his confidence, but struggled to maintain her calm. Something must be lost in translation – it wasn't possible that he was saying these things to her, was it?

"But," Jacopo began, his hands toying with the ends of the belt of his bathrobe, "wouldn't your job wait for you?"

"No," she said, and frowned. "It doesn't work like that at home. I wish it did."

He tilted his head and raised an eyebrow. "No?"

Emily shook her head. "If I don't come back when I said I would, they'll say I abandoned my job and hire someone else," she explained. "Someone cheaper," she added a moment later. "It wouldn't take much to provoke them, and I can't be that irresponsible. I have to go back to work and pay my bills. I've got to finish school and get my degree."

Jacopo said nothing, his gaze drifting toward the window.

"Besides," Emily added, with a sigh. "I couldn't afford to keep staying in that hotel. Or any other, really."

Jacopo's eyes shifted back to her, the corners of his mouth turning upward. "You would stay here. When Mamma returns, you would go to the guest room upstairs."

She laughed and played along. "I suppose we'd have to keep up appearances." *And we could make love on the sly*, she thought, and laughed again.

"*Sì, sì.* You would stay upstairs, and I would visit you each night."

Emily's laughter caught in her throat. *Dear God, I think he's serious.*

"I would visit you each night," Jacopo repeated, removing his robe and hooking the hood of it on one tall bedpost. "We would have to make love quietly, so Mamma would not hear us." He knelt on the bed once more, stalking slowly forward to pull the bedclothes out of her hands. Her fingers cramped, then released, the air cool on her hot palms as he smoothed the counterpane out on either side of her and guided her to lie back, beneath him.

He kissed her, soft and slow at first, but with increasing passion until she found herself wrapped around him with little recollection as to how it had happened. His own arousal was readily evident and he pressed closer to her, an echo of his teasing dance from the night before.

"Luckily for us, Mamma isn't here now," he murmured against her lips, and slipped inside her.

Emily gasped, both at the sentiment he'd expressed and in shock that he'd joined her without precautions. A protest rose to her lips and died as he surged forward, her hips rising in response. She moved eagerly against him, seeking her own pleasure this time, and he responded in kind, as though in appreciation of her efforts.

She bit back a small cry, the sound lodging in her throat after some effort, and Jacopo stopped to frame her face in his hands, his eyes boring into hers. "*Non resistere,*" he commanded, as she shuddered all around him. What he'd said was a mystery to her, but the intent was clear enough. "*Non resistere,*" he repeated, then resumed his thrusts until she shuddered again, crying out in release. "*Bellissima,*" he murmured into the curve of her shoulder, "*bellissima...*"

His sounds of pleasure, low grunts and growls of effort, short, clipped breaths when she moved a certain way, drove her forward. Helpless to resist, her fingers dug into his arms as she arced upward to meet his body with her own, a pained, pleading cry erupting from deep within her as she climaxed.

He followed suit a few moments later, his pleasure purring in his chest while he settled into her embrace. Lazily tangling his fingers in her hair, he nuzzled the side of her neck in a disarming, ticklish way.

Emily willed herself to calm, her dry throat to cease aching. Each breath she took, however, pulled in his musky scent and rekindled the sweet pulse keeping time with her heartbeat where he rested inside her, still ready to continue, it seemed.

He couldn't possibly be serious, could he? We barely know each other at all, to even suggest such a thing... He must have intended it to make this more exciting, a fantasy of sorts...

And what a fantasy it made. A Venetian lover in a palazzo on the Grand Canal? Who was she kidding? That was the sort of thing that happened to women like Jenn, not herself.

But Jenn isn't the one he's just made love to, is she? Last night he ignored her outright.

Emily opened her eyes and studied Jacopo's shoulder, the golden skin not quite so perfect, close-up. The imperfections were scarcely enough to matter, though; a few freckles spattered about and lurking beneath the even, cultured tan, a small scar that appeared as a crease in the smooth skin and that was all.

The fading ache between her thighs became a sharp throb at the thought. As if on cue, Jacopo drew away from her, sliding his body languorously across hers, leaving a warm trail over the cooling skin of her thigh. The scar on her abdomen shone a flushed, plastic pink, and she traced one finger along it. The slick surface beneath her fingertip didn't feel quite so disturbing, any more. A satisfied grin crept onto her lips with the thought.

Jacopo stilled until Emily thought he'd fallen asleep. Her own eyelids drooped in grateful fatigue before her stomach made a soft gurgle.

His chuckle beside her proved he was awake.

"We should have something for breakfast before I take you back to the hotel."

Emily nodded, surprised by her lack of disappointment.

"Okay," she said. "I'll just need to, um, freshen up a bit."

"Of course. It's to the right, at the end of the hall."

"Thanks." She stood and slipped her feet into her sandals, gathered her clothes and made her way to the door. She focused straight ahead on the doorway, her neck muscles tense, resisting the desire to turn and look back at him. The world swayed drunkenly for a moment and she rested her hand on the doorjamb as she stepped into the hall.

You have to breathe, you know.

One deep breath later she stood in the middle of an ultra-modern bathroom, surrounded by gleaming cream-colored tiles. Larger, pale-blue tiles on the floor radiated coolness in spite of the sunlight reflecting off them.

"You can put your clothes here," Jacopo said, startling her. She hadn't heard a single footstep behind her.

He took her clothes from her hands and hung them on the hooks on the back of the door, then smiled. She blushed, feeling more exposed than ever and her hands dithered by her sides. She was determined not to follow her instinct and cover herself in spite of the clear appraisal in his eyes. Absurd though it was, she didn't know where to look. Her eyes were drawn to follow every line of his naked body as he moved past her.

I had him. The thought was both startling and revelatory in its brashness. *I had him, and he still wants me. He wants* me.

She stood a little taller, a smile emerging as she did so.

"If you like, you could use these." He indicated a shelf of shampoos and shower gels in one corner of the large shower stall. "I think you'll find them pleasing, though it's a pity to hide your scent."

He stood next to her for a moment before he pressed against her. His body seemed even warmer in the coolness of the room. He bent and gave her shoulder an open-mouthed kiss, trailed his lips along her neck then nuzzled behind her ear and whispered, "You smell wonderful after you've made love, Emily. I would like to have your scent on me all day."

She gaped at him for a moment when he pulled away, then closed her mouth with an audible *snap.*

He trailed his gaze along her body once more, lingering with clear intent before he turned and left her alone. Her reflection in the tall mirror on the wall opposite the shower caught her eye and she turned, surprised at her appearance.

What was it he said the other day? "Come una donna di Botticelli?"

She watched her reflection and covered herself in a modest pose, à la Botticelli's "Birth of Venus." A soft giggle escaped her and her smile returned, stronger than before.

13

The ringing of the telephone echoed in the hallway, the sound amplified by the marble floors and bare walls. Emily finished dressing and listened to Jacopo's footfalls before his impatient "*Pronto?*" cut off the next ring.

While speaking rapidly into the phone, plain tones of protest crept into his voice. Emily stepped into the hallway and he turned to give her a half-hearted smile, tugging an ice-blue polo shirt down over his chest.

Emily went to a window and leaned against the frame, looking down into the courtyard and across the *rio* at the small *campo* beyond. It was early, yet, and the *campo* was empty except for a red tabby cat sunning itself in one corner.

"*Non c'è nessun'altro? Sei sicuro? Va bene...sì, sì...*" he said with a heavy sigh. The panicked-sounding voice on the line was loud enough for Emily to hear. "*Arrivo subito. Ciao. Ciao-ciao...*" Jacopo was still muttering farewells as he hung up the phone, shaking his head. He stared down at the phone for a moment before grumbling a final "*'fanculo*" at it.

"Hey, now. Even I know what *that* one means," Emily teased.

Jacopo looked up at her with an abashed grin. "*Scusa*, Emily. I'm sorry."

"Bad news?"

"No. Well, yes. I have to take care of some work today, so I won't be able to spend the day with you." He frowned and joined her at the window, slipping his arms tight around her. "I confess that I am disappointed with this."

"It can't be helped, I guess." Emily returned the embrace, her arms snug around his neck. "I'm just going to be packing and repacking, anyway. Maybe I'll take some more photos if there's time."

"You will take some of me?" he suggested, kissing her temple.

"Sure, if you want. I'd love to have some–" She stopped short. *Something to remember you by,* was what she'd nearly said. She cleared her throat to cover her error, and he squeezed her before letting her go.

"You could take some here," he said. "In my room, perhaps. I would prefer an informal portrait."

She forced a grin and hoped it looked sincere. "It's too bad I don't have my camera with me, now."

"Later, then," he said dismissively, and then glanced at the grandfather clock. "*Merda.* We have to go, now." He reached for her hand and she let him lead her down the hall to the front door.

She took a quick look around as they stepped out, wanting to commit it all to memory.

This time tomorrow, that's what it will be; a memory.

They stood at a tall table in the café, Jacopo with his *caffè ristretto*, Emily sipping her cappuccino. Though he had to go to work, he was certainly taking his time over the few drops of espresso in his tiny cup.

He'd selected pastries from the diminishing selection in the display case and now stood picking small pieces off the one he'd chosen, eating them one by one. From time to time, his eyes met hers and he smiled, and Emily's knees gave a little each time he did.

Watching his fingers nimbly shred the croissant or raise his cup to his lips, she had to hide a shiver at the memories of their lovemaking that morning and the night before. Yet again, she wondered why he had chosen her over Jenn. Reflecting on her friend's display with the *gelato* that night, perhaps she understood; but

Jacopo hadn't known this about Jenn when he'd chosen Emily, instead.

"*Amore*, tell me; what are you thinking?" he asked suddenly, and Emily shook her head, trying to dismiss her thoughts.

"Sorry?"

"What were you thinking, then? You were looking rather, *come si dice*... 'Puzzled?'" He sidled around the small tabletop to kiss her ear, and she smelled the strong coffee on his breath.

"Oh." She didn't continue, but turned her face up to his instead, expectantly.

Jacopo obliged her with another kiss and she tasted his coffee for herself, strong and bitter lacing his lips. Heedless of the other customers in the café, he parted her lips to slip his tongue past and tease her own before he pulled away.

"*Dimmi*," he whispered, sliding his arm around her waist and picking up her cappuccino to sample it. "Tell me."

Emily took a deep breath and met his gaze with hers, then plunged ahead.

"I was wondering why you chose me over Jenn."

He laughed aloud, drawing a glance from the *barista* and two older women seated on the bench by the door. "This is what you looked so serious for? *Dio bon!*"

"Well?" Emily felt the blush rise to her cheeks, a flash fire on her cool skin. "It doesn't make any sense, does it? Men follow her around everywhere she goes, and then the best of the bunch chooses me?"

"'Best of the bunch'?" Jacopo echoed, and her blush intensified. "Emily, *cara*..." he framed her face in his hands, still laughing. "This, I think, is your true flaw."

My face? she thought, and swallowed the goony laugh that threatened to erupt.

"You should have more confidence, *amore*. Men watch you, too. I promise this."

"Now who's not answering the question?"

"We have a saying, here: '*Dove la siesa è bassa, tuti passa.*' It means: 'Where the hedge is low, everybody passes.' Do you understand?"

Emily shook her head. "No, I don't. I'm sorry."

He sighed. "Okay. Your friend is a beautiful girl. But she is obvious about it. You are beautiful, but you aren't obvious about it. You stood out to me for that reason."

"When? When did I stand out to you?"

Jacopo regarded the café uneasily, his gaze moving from the doors to the *barista*, to the tabletop and back to Emily at last. "I was on the *vaporetto* with you when you arrived from the train station. Actually," he began, and cleared his throat before continuing, "I saw your friend first. You surprised me, though."

"I surprised you? How?"

He started to speak but fell silent. He bit his lower lip then licked it in a slow, pensive gesture. Emily's heart raced while she waited to hear his explanation, and she put down her cup before its chattering in its saucer could give her trembling away.

Jacopo moved closer to her again and bent to whisper in her ear, "I *wanted* you, Emily. As soon as I saw you, I wanted you."

Her hand went to the tabletop, gripping it hard to keep her feet. "No," she said, trying to sound flippant and certain that she'd failed. She looked up to find his earnest gaze meeting hers.

"*Sì, è vero, lo giuro*; it's true, I swear it." He shook his head in disbelief. "I have never before felt this so strongly. I lost you in Piazza San Marco and I stayed there hoping I'd see you two again. I was ready to give up when I went to that bar on the Molo and saw you come back from your gondola ride."

Oh, God... I didn't really believe him when he said he had been watching me.

"When I approached you, you walked away. I could have sworn that you saw me, before that."

"I did see you," Emily said, her voice scarcely a whisper as tears burned behind her eyes. "I thought you wanted Jenn."

"And I thought I shouldn't pursue you, then. How would you have reacted if I chased you down a *calle* to ask you out? I knew if I was alone with you I wouldn't be able to control myself, so I let you go." A rueful smile crossed his lips and he shook his head. "When I saw you at the shop the next morning, I decided that I had to take the chance. Better you should turn me down than to give up too soon."

"You *were* resisting pretty well, Jacopo. I still don't understand why, either." If only for something to do, Emily sipped her cold cappuccino. She stared at the half-empty cup. "You could have had me that first night," she murmured, and he leaned in closer. "You could have, but you didn't. Why not?"

"I was afraid of what I was feeling." He shrugged in a sheepish effort that barely registered in her peripheral vision. "I was afraid of what I wanted, and of dragging you into this."

"Into what?"

"*Mamma*," he said simply, and moved his gaze toward the window.

"I don't understand," she said, and put her hand over his where it rested on the tabletop. "You mean because she's sick?"

"I mean because she's dying. That, and she... You know." He shook his head again and took Emily's hand in his. "She's relentless. I didn't want you to suffer that."

"She seemed harmless enough, to me."

Jacopo frowned. "She's not, though."

"Well, I know a thing or two about relentless mothers, remember?"

He raised Emily's hand to his lips and kissed the palm gently, nodding. "We'd better go. I have to work."

At the hotel, Emily had scarcely asked for her room key before Jenn came bustling down the hall, her expression a mix of excitement and relief. As she stepped into reception and saw Jacopo, however, she stopped short, looking startled.

Jacopo's hand on Emily's shoulder drew her attention back to him.

"*Amore*, I have to go," he said, stroking her cheek. "I'm already late."

"Okay," Emily said softly, leaning into his touch.

"I'll come by this evening, all right?"

He cupped her cheek as she nodded in response, and bent to give her a surprisingly chaste kiss on the lips. His eyes told an altogether different story, however, and Emily felt an immodest rush of heat all over.

"*Ciao*, Emily," Jacopo said, raising his hand in Jenn's direction. "Jenn."

"*Ciao*," Emily said, hearing her friend's echoed response a second later. She turned to face her, eager to share details of the night before, but her expectant smile died on her lips.

Uncharacteristic frown lines around Jenn's mouth somehow accented the darker circles of skin beneath her eyes, making her look both exhausted and unhappy. Emily froze, fearing the worst, and forced herself to go to her.

"Has something happened?"

"I was beginning to wonder that, myself." Jenn's tone was cold enough to raise the fine hairs on Emily's arms.

"What do you mean?" she asked, and Jenn turned on her heel to march back to her room.

Emily watched her go.

"*Signorina*? Your key," the clerk offered politely.

Taking the key in hand, Emily gave him a weary, embarrassed smile. "*Grazie*."

"If I may?" the clerk asked, leadingly, and she nodded permission. "Your friend, she asked many times last night if you had called for her. I think she was concerned."

"*Grazie*, again," Emily said, and sighed. She turned to go as the clerk sat back on his stool, switching on the tiny TV behind the counter.

Emily stood in front of Jenn's door for what felt like forever before she was ready to knock. She considered going to her own room instead, but knew it wasn't really an option. This was her best friend throwing a fit before a full day of travel together. If she let this slide, she'd have to deal with cold silence all the way home.

Before her knuckles could strike the wood, she heard Jenn's resigned, "I can hear you out there, so just come on in."

Emily opened the door just enough to peer inside and better assess Jenn's temperament. Her long legs were drawn up to her chest, her arms folded tight around them, and her eyes were hooded with fatigue. It was obvious she hadn't slept well the previous night.

A flicker of guilt flared and gutted almost at once. Emily stepped inside, closing the door behind her. "What's going on, Sissy?"

"Not much. So; you were with him, then?"

Emily nodded, trying not to smile at the thought. "Yeah, I was."

"Hm…" Jenn's gaze focused on the rumpled bedclothes at her feet. "I was worried."

"I'm sorry."

"I mean I was *really* worried, Mouse. This wasn't like you."

"I know," Emily said, and shrugged, trying to dislodge her growing resentment. "I guess I was due for a change, huh? The mouse has become a raging muskrat." She cast a sidelong glance at Jenn, hoping for a smile, but found none. "Well, you can stop worrying, anyway. I'm here; I'm fine. See?"

"Yeah, well… You don't know what I felt when I got up this morning and you weren't here. No note, no message, nothing at all; I started imagining having to explain to your mother what had happened to you…"

Jenn shivered visibly and Emily felt a brief regret before she banished it.

"I didn't think it would bother you that much."

"You could have called. You *should* have called."

"Oh. Like you always do? Wait, I'm sorry – that's never happened, has it?"

Jenn's eyes barely raised from their bleary focus on the bed.

Emily stood and crossed to the window. The view of the dock below was much better than from her room, she noted.

"There was never a good time to call, anyway." She gritted her teeth before she could say anything like an apology. "You must have guessed what was going to happen when we left the *gelateria*. What did you think we were going to do?"

"If his track record was any indication," Jenn began, each word dripping sarcasm, "I guess I thought he'd blue-ball again."

Emily spun around, mouth agape. "For crying out loud! I should think you'd be happy for me, for once."

"It's still no reason for you to disappear like that."

"Holy shit – you're jealous!"

"I am *not*."

"You *are*. Why else would you be upset with me over this, when you've done it a million times?"

"A *million* times?"

"Give or take a couple *thousand*, yeah, maybe."

Jenn burst into tears. Emily froze again, stunned.

What the hell?

She crossed over to the bed and sat down gingerly. "I'm sorry. I didn't mean it."

"Yes, you did. I suppose I deserved that, though."

"Well... Yes, and no." Emily grinned and looked at Jenn, finding a sad half-grin in response. "But why now? Why aren't you happy for me? I finally got that fun I've been looking for, you know?"

Jenn nodded and wiped her eyes with the back of her hand. "I *am* happy for you, Mou– Emily," she said, correcting herself. "Really, I am. I guess I just didn't expect it, or something."

"Yeah, well. Neither did I, until it was happening."

"So... it happened, last night? For real?"

Emily shrugged. "Nah. Blue-balls again."

"What?" Genuine surprise filled Jenn's face.

"Just kidding," Emily said, laughing. "Seriously, though; something happened, Jenn. Something big."

"'Big', how?" Jenn asked, then sniggered a moment later. "Sorry, I took that the wrong way."

"Pervert." Emily giggled, relief flooding her at last. "I mean something really big." She covered her face with her hands for a moment and took a deep breath. "Something huge."

Jenn drew back, her eyes narrowing. "What happened, Em?"

"He asked me if I wanted to stay longer – in Venice, I mean."

"Really? Oh. Oh, my God."

"My thoughts, exactly." A slow blush crept up, warming Emily's face, and she pressed her hands to her face to cool it. "But that's not all..." she said, her voice trailing off as her eyes misted over.

"No? What is it?" Jenn studied Emily's face and put her arm around her.

"He thinks I'm *beautiful*, Jenn. He really does."

Jenn hugged her close and sighed, then laughed. "Of course he does, Em. You *are* beautiful; I've been telling you that forever."

"Then why didn't I feel it, before?"

"Because you didn't *believe* it, before." Jenn laughed again. "It's about time you finally did."

14

Jacopo picked up the cardboard tube that had lain neglected on the desk from the day he'd given it to her. He tapped his fingers along the length absentmindedly, as if trying to make a decision. Emily continued folding her clothes, watching him out of the corner of her eye while he examined the package.

"You haven't opened it," he said, a statement instead of a question.

"No, I haven't."

"Why not?"

Emily permitted herself a shrug and went on packing clothes in her suitcase. "I'm waiting for the right moment?"

Jacopo placed the tube back on the desk and opened the window. "And when might that be, Emily?" He crossed the room to stand beside her. "Before or after you leave Venezia?"

"I hadn't thought about it, really."

He framed her face in his hands and kissed her with an intense, hungry effort until she dropped her handful of clothes atop the open suitcase on the bed. She felt him smiling through the kiss even before he drew away and she could see it for herself.

He seemed about to speak, but instead kissed her again. His arms were tight around her so she had to struggle to put her arms around his neck and press against the length of him. His own warmth and the heat of the day intensified where they touched, and Emily moved against him, savoring the heat and craving more.

"Emily..." he murmured against the curve of her neck, and she shivered as his breath cooled on her skin.

"Hmm?" she answered wordlessly, her lips brushing against his ear, gratified to feel his own shiver follow. She initiated the next kiss, this one long and deep. His hands stole furtively over her clothes, then pushed the fabric aside to stroke and caress the skin beneath. When he pulled away, her body followed as though of its own accord, unwilling to give up the contact.

This time is my turn. She held him close and pressed her lips to his throat, her tongue slipping over his Adam's apple and downward to the top button of his shirt.

His appreciative sigh was soft in the room as she tugged his shirt upward with impatient fingers. He managed to pull the garment over his head before she began undoing his belt with fumbling, frantic energy. She pushed his trousers over his hips more roughly than she'd intended, and Jacopo gave a rueful laugh before he finished undressing on his own, one hand out as if warding her off.

Emily felt the familiar shudder low in her belly as she traced her hands over his body in a slow demonstration of willpower. The drunken feeling raged back into her, strong enough to make her dizzy but no less excited by Jacopo's evident arousal in her hands. She slipped to her knees, still grasping and stroking him eagerly, before she brought her mouth to him in a slow kiss.

"...*Oddio*..." Jacopo rolled his hips forward, his hands twining in her hair, encouraging more. She obliged, her hands and mouth returning to him time and again in fleeting, delirious feasting until he drew swiftly away.

She was unfastening her skirt when he raised her to her feet and pushed her onto the bed, dismissing with any further delay. The suitcase thumped to the floor, spilling its contents, and Jacopo shoved aside the folded stacks of clothing so they followed behind. He grasped her hips and grappled with her panties, pulling them roughly downward, the fabric rolling up as he tugged the garment down her thighs.

He tossed the garment aside without a glance, his gaze focused on her face, watching and gauging her reactions. His lips curled into a smile and he grasped her breast, his other hand bunching her skirt up out of the way before he parted her thighs and thrust one knee between them.

She reached to undo her bra, and he pushed her down onto her back, his fingers making short work of pushing the straps aside and wresting the fabric down to expose her skin to his fervent, probing lips and tongue. He sucked at one nipple, pulling it with his teeth just hard enough that she twitched away from him and made a little squeak of pain.

"*Mi dispiace, tesoro mio...*" he whispered against the smarting, protesting flesh, then trailed the flat of his tongue over it in a soothing gesture.

She arched her back, her fingers twined in his hair, tangling in the damp blond waves as he continued lapping at her nipple, teasing her at his leisure. She tightened her grip in his hair, pulling him down onto her breast, silently demanding more.

He smelled impossibly good. Emily licked her lips, imagining drinking him in. Her tongue worked uselessly in her mouth to coax his taste deeper inside. He moved against her, matching the eager, restless motion of her hips as she rubbed against his thigh.

With another abrupt movement, he spread her thighs wider and slipped between them, pressing against her in his familiar, teasing way. It was a maddening caress, toying with her need and eagerness while he held her in place and refused her any release.

She was still so very close, all the same.

One hand remained tangled in his hair, and she lowered the other to his waist, digging her fingers into the tender flesh just above his hip. His short, shocked inhalation showed she had his attention, now.

"Emily..." his voice was a low growl, barely out of his chest.

"Jacopo..." her own voice was a rasping murmur, much the same as his.

He raised one eyebrow in obvious puzzlement for a moment before his usual sly confidence returned.

"Don't move, *tesoro*... Be still."

"No." Speaking the word sent a surge of strength through her. Her skin tingled at the sight of genuine surprise in his face, and she took advantage of his momentary confusion to push him off her and onto his back. Before he could even speak, she swung one leg over to crouch astride him without taking him in.

His eyes widened in incomprehension before a broad smile spread across his lips. Faster than she would have believed possible, his hands swept under her skirt to grasp her thighs and hold her in place. When he raised his hips, she shifted as best she could, evading him.

His grip on her thighs tightened and she froze, wondering vaguely if she would find bruises there later.

"Be *still*...," he whispered, and her previously afflicted nipple throbbed in time with the pulse between her thighs.

They remained frozen for what felt like an eternity, until her leg muscles began to quake and quiver, threatening to give out from under her. Where her skirt didn't cover his arms, she saw his muscles flexing and tensing, too, trembling like guy wires in a high wind.

She closed her eyes and gave in, surrendering to her own desire to complete the act they were dancing so determinedly around. To her surprise, he seemed to do the same.

He slipped inside her easily, drawing her legs close after she'd settled comfortably atop him. With a tender caress, he brushed her hair back from her face into a messy ponytail, which he held loosely in one hand as he kissed her mouth.

Emily pressed against him, tentatively rocking her hips to take him deeper inside herself. He rose to meet her efforts, slowly at first, then with increasing speed.

Soon his thrusts were swift and forceful, rough enough to rock her forward atop him while the bed frame itself quailed and complained beneath. Emily heard herself crying out as though from a distance, and the sound of Jacopo's exhalations were enough to push her to the brink.

It was his grunted "*Vengo!*" that sent her over. There was no question of what it meant, now – she felt him swelling inside her, pulsing in time with her orgasm when he came and pulling hard on her hips, striving to go deeper still before she collapsed upon him in slow stages.

His breathing was unsteady as she rested atop him, and she closed her eyes, willing herself to remember the moment, to remember what it was like to make love with this sort of passion. It surely wouldn't happen again.

"Emily? Oh... *Oddio...*" Jacopo drew back, brushed her hair away from her face once again and delicately wiped away the tears that streamed down her cheeks. "*Cos'è successo?* Have I hurt you?"

She couldn't resist the chuckle that bubbled up at his concern, but slowly rolled off him to look up at the ceiling.

"No, no you haven't," she reassured him.

"Then what is the matter?"

"Nothing, Jacopo. I promise. Nothing's wrong."

His eyes narrowed, his fingers still stroking her cheek where the tears had dried, smeared by his touch.

"What are you thinking, Emily? I think I see something in your eyes, but I cannot read it."

She turned to face him and met his gaze with her own for a long, silent moment.

"That would be happiness, Jacopo. And sadness, too."

"*Perché?*" his brow furrowed as Emily raised an eyebrow in confusion. "Why?" he translated. "Why are you happy and sad?"

"I'm happy because no one has ever made me feel this good before," she said with a grin, and watched an echoing smile curl Jacopo's lips for an instant.

"And sad...?"

"Because..." She hesitated, uncertain if she should tell him. "Because I'm going to miss you."

The blankness came over his expression once again and he lay down next to her without another word.

Emily lay still for a few moments before she reached to push her skirt down to cover her thighs, then adjusted her bra to ease the discomfort where the elastic seemed to have tightened around her torso. She watched him again, unsure of what she hoped to find.

Jacopo was quiet enough to convince her that he'd drifted off to sleep. Entranced by the rise and fall of his chest, Emily reached out and traced her fingertips from his navel up to his throat, relishing the warmth of him beneath her touch.

"I'm sorry," she whispered.

She startled when he grasped her hand in his own and held it against him. His eyes remained closed as he let her feel his heart beating underneath her palm.

"Emily, I must confess something..."

"What is it?" she asked slowly, hoping to avoid sounding too curious.

"It is not easy for me to see you go." He opened his eyes and met hers, his direct gaze unnerving. "Do you understand that?"

"I have to admit, it's a bit puzzling. We've only known each other a couple of days, really."

"And yet I've offered you a place to stay, if you wished to. Why didn't you accept?"

"You were serious?"

"Of course I was," Jacopo said in a tone people normally reserved for reassuring a child. He shook his head with something like disbelief and grasped her hand tighter in his own. "So why not stay?"

"I..." Emily's thoughts stuttered in her mind, unable to decide which path to take. "Jacopo, I can't do that."

He sat up, pulling her up with him. "Be reasonable, Emily."

Reasonable?

"Jaco—"

"Emily," he cut her off, his voice abrupt and loud in the confines of the hotel room. He softened a moment later, his grasp of her hand relaxing while he brushed her hair out of her eyes with the other hand. "Emily, you must understand this, too: you make me feel different than any of my other girlfriends did. What happened here today has never happened in this way, before. I've certainly never asked any of them to stay with me in my home. *Perdio!* Until you, I've never even made love without a condom before."

Emily felt her eyes open wide. "Really?"

A faint blush rose in his chest and face and he looked away from her. "No, never."

"Well, I... Never mind that. You should know I feel the same way. Honestly, I've never enjoyed being with someone so much - but it's only been a couple of days! What you're asking is impossible."

"*Impossibile?*" he asked, spinning the word into its Italian counterpart. "No, it is not. You just have to be willing to take the chance. Besides, it's not that I am asking it forever."

Emily smiled. *At least he's honest.*

"I wish I could, Jacopo. But I have a home, and a job, to go back to."

"It's not much of a job; you've said so yourself."

"It's the only job I have, though," she said. "I can't take for granted that I'll find another one later. It's taken me a while to get to where I can go to school and work without juggling schedules and –" She shook her head to clear it. "That's not the point, anyway. We hardly know each other."

"Marriages are founded on less," he countered, stroking her palm with his fingertips.

"We're not talking about marriage, though, are we? We're talking about...I don't know what we're talking about."

"We are talking about taking time for us. We are talking about taking advantage of an opportunity that we have been given." Jacopo brought her hand to his lips and brushed a light kiss over her palm. "We are talking about making love to one another and being together as long as we desire to be. Not everyone has that chance, Emily."

She bit her lip and remained silent, still struggling to focus and think.

This is insanity. This is a purple-prose pulp novel come to life. It can't be real, either way.

"Just consider it, Emily. This is all I ask." The tinge of defeat in Jacopo's voice, before he released her hand and got up from the bed, was enough to give her pause.

He dressed at a leisurely pace, without the slightest hint of hurry or embarrassment. Once dressed, he went to the desk and picked up the cardboard tube. He turned it end over end in his hands, his fingertips examining the intact seals, his gaze focusing out of the open window for a few moments.

Emily slipped back into her blouse, now too rumpled to wear outside, and watched him from the bed until he turned to face her. He crossed to the bed, holding the tube out before him so she would take it, and she did.

"Open it, Emily," he said, his voice warmer and gentler than she'd ever heard it.

He left without another word.

15

Emily didn't need to see the bags beneath her eyes – she felt them there, swollen, containing the bulk of a restless night. The sleepless hours she'd passed alone were nearly enough to convince her that she'd started losing her mind.

The cardboard tube rested next to her as it had since Jacopo left, still unopened despite the loving caresses she'd imparted from time to time. Emily reviewed his giving of this gift over and over again, trying to guess what it might contain. She was certain it was one of the prints that had fascinated her in the shop, and this mattered, for some strange reason she couldn't quite fathom. She desperately wanted to guess the contents before opening the tube, but didn't know why.

It was just a little gift, right? Nothing special about it.

Except for what he'd said, when he gave it to her; "I just thought you should have it, after I saw you admiring it in the shop."

How did he see me looking at the prints? I was talking to the old man when Jacopo came in – I could swear it.

The prints had been lovely, though. One, of a bridge to the square where the shop itself stood; the other, a watercolor of Proserpina eating the pomegranate seeds that would confine her to Hades.

So which was it? The bridge, or Proserpina? Proserpina or the bridge?

The question echoed in her head, an all-consuming thought, until at last the sun shone on the buildings across the canal, and she slept and dreamed.

On the way to the water taxi stand in front of the train station, Emily paused in the piazza, turning to face the Grand Canal. Jenn returned belatedly to where she stood and gazed out at the canal, as well.

"What is it? One last look before we go?"

Emily didn't answer and the rumbling of an approaching *vaporetto* filled the silence. She scanned the canal, watching for Jacopo's runabout in hopes that perhaps he would come to try to persuade her to stay. He'd seemed so disappointed the night before, though. Most likely she had convinced him in spite of herself.

Still, she hadn't realized how much she really wanted to stay, until now. *If he asked me again...* she thought, and another realization struck her as her vision tunneled into shades of gray.

"Proserpina," Emily said, her voice dreamlike to her own ears as she fought the desire to give in and swoon. Breathing deeply, she forced herself to focus on the world around her. It was real, and she knew without a doubt that she was right; Jacopo knew which prints she'd looked at, because he had watched her through the paper shop.

"What?"

"It's Proserpina, eating the pomegranate seeds."

Jenn's furrowed brow repeated the question for her, and Emily ignored her friend to drop the suitcase onto the pavement to unfasten the latches. The cardboard tube was close to the top. Emily drew it out quickly, slipping a fingernail under the tape on one end to slice it open.

"Emily? What's going on?"

Glancing up at her friend, Emily didn't answer, but shook the tightly-rolled print out of the cardboard sleeve into her hand. The purple silk ribbon gleamed softly in the dull light of the overcast sky, and Emily tugged at the bow to untie it.

She heard it as she had the first time. The supple, liquid sound of the ribbon sliding against itself and against the parchment paper was like a friendly whisper amongst the comings-and-goings of travelers from the station. It resonated in her memory as well, in the *campo* outside the paper shop, while Jacopo stood close at hand to see how she would receive her gift.

The memory of the scent of his cologne on the breeze made her breathe in, seeking it once more before she licked her lips and swallowed hard.

It only took a glance at the print to know she was right. The image was of Proserpina, plucking the seeds from the pomegranate with a dreaming half-smile on her lips. The pomegranate itself was held in the palm of Plutone's hand, offered lovingly for her to accept or reject. She accepted willingly.

Emily smiled. It corresponded with her version of the myth, in the end.

"I see," he'd said. "I'd take care of this."

"He didn't mean that I should handle Mom. He meant that *he'd* do it."

Jenn's brow furrowed in deeper confusion. "What are you talking about?"

Emily looked up at her best friend, smiling more broadly than before. "I'm sorry. I've had a change of plan."

Jenn crouched down next to Emily, resting one hand on Emily's shoulder for support. She glanced at the print before Emily rolled it up and tucked it back into its container.

"What are you talking about? What's going on?"

Emily closed the suitcase and latched it shut. "I'm not coming with you."

"You're taking your own water taxi? Em, that's really expensive, and risky, too. You're bound to miss the plane."

"I know," Emily said, standing. "I intend to."

Jenn's eyes grew wide and she stood up to clutch Emily's arm. "What do you mean?"

Emily shook her off gently, reaching back to tie her hair into a ponytail with the purple silk ribbon. "I'll call Mom and explain it to her before you even get home."

"Explain it to *me*, first, okay?"

"I'm staying here. With Jacopo." Emily pursed her lips thoughtfully. "That is, if he hasn't changed his mind. If he has, I'll be on the next flight home." She shrugged, the gesture light and carefree. "You don't have to worry about me, though. I'll be fine."

"Emily Miller? Have you lost your mind?"

She laughed aloud at the bewildered look on Jenn's face. "No, I haven't. I'm going to take a chance for once, that's all." Emily reached out and grabbed Jenn in a warm hug. "Wish me luck, okay?"

"You're crazy," Jenn said and sighed, returning the embrace. "I just hope you know what you're doing."

"We'll see, won't we?" Emily released Jenn and grabbed the suitcase, already plotting her course. "I'll call you ASAP. I promise."

"Okay. Just don't leave me to face your mother's wrath – you know she'll blame it all on me."

"She should, anyway – it's all your fault." Emily laughed, then turned to hurry down the steps toward the dock and the approaching *vaporetto*. "You said I should have an adventure. I'm just doing what I was told."

A lopsided smile crossed Jenn's face, almost canceling out the puzzlement there, and she raised one hand to wave goodbye. Emily did the same, then boarded the *vaporetto* without looking back.

Emily stood in front of the wooden bridge over the *rio* in front of Jacopo's palazzo, wiped her palms on her jeans and pressed the intercom call button. The bell rang deep inside the palazzo's foyer, breaking the silence of the *campo*.

She waited a moment then rang again, noting that the sound came from the open window above the large front door, the one with the winged lion over it.

He might not be home. Maybe he's at work, today? But no, it's a Saturday, that wouldn't be too likely —

A light-haired figure in dark clothing went past the window where she'd heard the sound of the bell, but she couldn't tell if it was Jacopo or not. The lacy curtains drifted in and out of the window, obscuring her view of the main corridor. A loud crackling from the speaker beneath the call button gave her a start, drawing her attention away from the windows of the palazzo.

"*Chi è?*" Jacopo's voice demanded, and Emily paused before speaking.

"It's me," she said.

"*Chi?*" came the louder, more insistent response and for a moment it seemed there was another voice speaking at the same time.

"It's me," Emily said, louder now, and glanced over the gate, up to the open window, to catch a glimpse of Jacopo looking out. His wide eyes and gape of surprise were evident even at a distance. Emily raised one hand and gave him a small, timid wave, fighting a rush of disappointment as he vanished from the window.

Jacopo didn't return to the intercom. A soft click over the speaker was all Emily heard, followed by silence. She waited, shivering in spite of the early August heat, her gaze still trained on the open window, while she listened for any sound of activity in the palazzo.

None came.

Oh, my God... I totally misread everything. He didn't want me to do this at all.

Her fingers felt numb, gripping the cardboard tube until it was slick from the nervous perspiration of her hand. She resisted the urge to run, senselessly and without direction, and moved to stand with the stone column between herself and the palazzo.

Dizziness swept over her and she swayed on her feet, steadying herself with one hand against the stones.

I have to go. I can make it to the airport in time for the next flight, surely.

She grasped the handle of her suitcase and turned away, her heart thudding sickeningly low, making her nauseous. She forced her feet to move, but it was like wading through surf up to her knees. Every step was unsteady, the ground shifting beneath her feet.

The sudden buzz and *clack* behind her seemed distant, as though farther along the *rio*, and she didn't dare turn back.

I'll just be disappointed again. Why ask for a kick when I'm down?

"Emily."

She stopped, already nearly halfway across the tiny *campo*, and peered back over her shoulder.

Jacopo stood at the open gate, the expression of disbelief still on his face.

"I thought you were leaving today."

She glanced down at her suitcase then turned to face him. "I was supposed to. I thought I might stay a little longer, though. That is, um..." She swallowed hard and took a deep breath. "That is, if a certain offer still stands."

Jacopo stood silent and unmoving for an eternity. He glanced back at the palazzo and then pushed a broken brick with his foot to keep the gate propped open.

He walked swiftly toward her, crossing to the middle of the *campo* in a few paces, and took her suitcase in hand.

"Wait right here," he said quietly.

He returned to the gate, crossed the bridge and disappeared behind the wooden door that led to the courtyard. She could hear the door to the palazzo itself open and close quickly before he strode across the little bridge toward her once more, reaching for her hand.

He drew her to himself and held her close, his hand slipping up her back to tug at her ponytail in a quick, playful gesture. Brushing loose strands of hair back from her face and tucking them behind her ears with both hands, he bent to kiss her, his lips pulling and stroking hers tenderly.

"I tried to call, but you'd already left the hotel," he said at last. "I didn't know which *vaporetto* you were going to take, so... Then my employer called me and I couldn't get away." He exhaled a deep breath, closed his eyes and pressed his forehead to hers, his arms tight around her waist. "I had just about made up my mind to call the airlines."

The swooning sensation swept over Emily again and she tightened her arms around his neck even though she didn't need to — he was holding her up well enough. Her breath caught in her chest, wrapped around a sob in the depths of her throat. She gulped down a shallow breath and felt the sting of tears in the corners of her eyes.

"All of them?" she asked, when she could finally speak again.

Jacopo chuckled deep in his chest and hummed a tone of reassurance. "Every last one, *tesoro mio*."

She looked up at him, feeling the first tear spill over and hoping he'd understand why it did. "What does that mean? *'Tesoro mio'*?" she asked as he brushed the tear away with the backs of his fingers.

"It means 'my Treasure,' *amore*." He kissed her again and she felt her pulse throbbing hard, and she knew he felt it too. "Come with me," he said, taking her hand again and leading her away from the gate.

"Where are we going?"

"We're going for lunch," he said. "I know a wonderful place. You're going to love it."

"But don't you need to tell them you're going?"

"Tell who?" Jacopo glanced back at his palazzo quickly, concern flitting across his face.

"Your guest. Wasn't there someone with you? I heard another voice on the intercom. At least," she amended, with a strange sense of guilt, "I thought I did, anyway."

He gave her a look somewhere between confusion and frustration, still leading her along.

"Oh, right. That was the — ah, *come si dice?* — the maid. Yes. The maid is in, today."

They'd nearly reached the far end of the empty *campo* when he suddenly stepped in front of her and framed her face in his hands. He seemed momentarily distracted, swiftly surveying their surroundings before his gaze returned to study her features attentively. He lowered his mouth to hers, hovering for an instant before brushing lightly over her lips, then pressed closer with clearer intent.

She put her arms around his neck, distantly aware that her skin seemed almost tan against his white shirt in the afternoon light. She tried to lose herself in his kiss, remembering the first one they'd shared on the bridge just a few nights ago.

Not-so-distantly, the sound of a heavy wooden door opening and shutting, followed by the careful closing of an iron gate, carried across the *campo* at her back. He stopped kissing her and drew her close once more, his embrace tighter than she'd expected it to be.

Emily pressed her face to his chest, ignoring the sound of high-heeled footsteps disappearing down the *calle* and the seed of self-doubt they planted close to her heart, next to the jasmine perfume in Jacopo's shirt.

Her choice was made.

Thanks and Acknowledgements

I have many people to thank for helping me with the writing of this story. The first draft was completed with the help of both my critique partner Nell Dixon and my editor Jason Horger. Without them, the story would never have taken shape or come to fruition.

I also owe a huge debt to my beta readers who pointed out the little slip-ups which got past my jaded eye. To Deborah Surman-Hobbs, Jarrah Dale, Kimberley Troutte, Heikki Hietala and Terhi Ikonen, I give my sincere and heartfelt thanks.

Finally, I can honestly say that I'd never have gotten this story finished without the music of several Italian artists at hand, including Samuele Bersani, Subsonica, Gianna Nannini and Baustelle. Their work fuelled the mood on these pages and helped me find my "groove" when I needed to keep going and found myself faltering.

And finally, I owe a huge thanks to my husband, Alessandro, who inspires me and supports me in my writing efforts, as well as checks my Italian (most of it, anyway). So, any errors you find in these pages are mine and mine alone.

About the Author

An aspiring writer from the age of eight, Kimberly Menozzi began writing her first stories instead of paying attention in school. While her grades might have suffered, her imagination seldom did. She managed to keep most of her stories together for years, then lost them after a move when she left a trunk full of papers behind. (She meant to go back and get them, but circumstances prevented her from doing so.)

So, she started over again. And lost those, too.

After a trip to England in 2002, she began work on *A Marginal Life (Well-Lived)*, inspired by the music of Jarvis Cocker and Pulp. The novel was completed in 2003, and is undergoing rewrites with hopes of publication in the near future.

Also in 2003, she met and fell in love with an Italian accountant named Alessandro. She married him in 2004. This necessitated her arrival in Italy and she has lived there ever since. After several months of working for language schools and writing blog entries for her family in the US to read, new story ideas began to develop.

Finally, in 2007, she began work on a new project, inspired by her love/hate relationship with her new home. The novel *Ask Me if I'm Happy* was completed in August of 2009 and was released on November 15th, 2010.

Kimberly is presently at work on her next project, due for release in 2013. *27 Stages* is a romantic novel set in the world of professional road cycling.

Connect with Kimberly Online:

Kimberly's website: http://www.kmenozzi.com

Kimberly on Twitter: http://twitter.com/KMenozzi

Kimberly on Facebook:
https://www.facebook.com/authorkmenozzi

Kimberly's blog: http://www.kmenozzi.com/blog.html

www.ingramcontent.com/pod-product-compliance
Lightning Source LLC
Chambersburg PA
CBHW030539130626
46552CB00006B/2334

* 9 7 8 0 6 1 5 4 9 1 5 6 1 *